The Devil and Mrs Baker
Borderliners Writers' Group

Published in 2014 by FeedARead.com Publishing

Copyright © The authors as named on the book cover.

First Edition

The authors have asserted their moral right under the Copyright, Designs and Patents Act, 1988, to be identified as the author of this work.

All Rights reserved. No part of this publication may be reproduced, copied, stored in a retrieval system, or transmitted, in any form or by any means, without the prior written consent of the copyright holder, nor be otherwise circulated in any form of binding or cover other than that in which it is published and without a similar condition being imposed on the subsequent purchaser.

A CIP catalogue record for this title is available from the British Library.

*For Brian Roberts -
a friend and fellow writer.
Aways in our hearts.*

Introduction

Welcome to the third anthology from The Borderliners.

The group has its origins in a West Cheshire College writing course held in the former Borders bookshop in Ellesmere Port, Cheshire. Sandwiched between shelves of books ranging from engineering to embroidery, class members produced and shared work which displayed an impressive variety of subject matter and writing styles

Eventually, an independent writing group developed and became known as The Borderliners, continuing to meet at the bookshop until its closure in 2009.

Since then, the group has continued to meet weekly at The Rake in Little Stanney. Meetings are friendly, fun and supportive. The work offered within this collection reflects the diversity and talents of the writers.

As with previous anthologies, all proceeds from this collection will be donated to charity.

Acknowledgements

We would like to thank the staff and management at The Rake for allowing us to meet at their premises, also family and friends who have wittingly and unwittingly provided us with inspiration.

Compiled by Chris Stork
Cover photograph by Sandra Johnson

Borderliners can be contacted at
borderlinerwriters@gmail.com

Contents

Sandra Johnson
The Devil and Mrs Baker	8
Crossed Lines	16
The Gift	21

Trevor K. Bell
A Forest Tale	25

Anne Abbinnett
Calling Time	31
Communication Breakdown	34
The Answer's in the Stars	39
Homeless	41
Leap of Faith	42
Memories	47

Doug Barratt
Cyril's Journey	49
A Magic Night	55

Lynne Stokoe
A Walk Across the Bay	59
Happy Heart	60
Hope	62
Oswald's Story	65
Spaced Out	69
The Village at the End of the World	70

Peter Scarisbrick
Alan's Art   74
Compromise   79
Lawrence (of Arabia)   84

Christine Milliken
An Organised Affair   85
Forbidden Love   90

John Edwards
Life's Full of Surprises   96
Memories   99
We Nearly Got Rich   101

Annette Hayes
Coffee Time   104
Payback   108
Strawberry Tarts   113

Mike Freeman
If Music be the Food of Love   116
The Restaurant   121
The Volunteer   123
Mind Me   125
The Village Bonfire   126

Helen Barratt
Julia   128
Up, Up and Away   131

Chris Stork
The Mad Queen of the Pier   135

Brian D. Roberts
Garrulous Hordes   143

Sandra Johnson
The Devil and Mrs Baker

Mrs Baker arranged the church flowers every Friday, and today was Friday. She opened up the side door which led into a little anteroom where the vicar usually changed into his cassock and delving into her bottomless bag pulled out a lilac overall, secateurs, rubber gloves and all the dizzying paraphernalia required by a professional flower arranger. Staggering up the aisle with her load, she deposited the instruments one by one, like a surgeon, on a pew.

Smoothing a wipe clean tablecloth over the altar, she then laid an array of flowers and greenery in a regimented heap, and with great skill began arranging the blooms into various receptacles. Humming softly to herself, *'Rock of Ages Cleft for me, let me hide myself in Thee.'*

She completed her task and was walking up the aisle with a vase of lilies when a bloodcurdling shriek cut the atmosphere. Mrs Baker dropped the vase in shock as the sound ripped through her head. She had never heard anything this loud since 1983 when she was standing next to the choir the day Mrs Pinnington attempted to add a soprano harmony to *'Men of Harlech.'*

Mrs Baker stood frozen with terror, water dripping down her skirt, her shoes were drenched, splintered glass littered the tiles and flowers lay broken at her feet. Then everything was still. The scream had been unearthly. It was the sound of a demon. The sound of the devil.

Finally recovering her senses, and with trembling legs, she fled from the church leaving the lights blazing, the flowers scattered and the door gaping. She ran sobbing and stumbling through the churchyard, her clothes catching on branches and bracken and didn't stop until heaving and breathless, she quivered on the steps of the crumbling rectory.

༄

Trevor the Revver, as he was known by his diminished flock, because of his propensity to drive his Morris Traveller at twenty-five miles per hour – everywhere - even on motorways, was awoken with a start by the ringing of the door bell and the pounding of his knocker. Jumping up, his unfinished sermon slipping to the floor, along with three half-completed crossword puzzles, he made haste to the door. In fell a wet, dishevelled, sobbing Mrs Baker. It took a full five minutes and a cup of sweet tea and three *Hobnobs* to finally wring the facts out of her gasping lips.
   'A ghost... the devil... in the church.'
   Never had he seen her in such a state. What could have possibly caused such hysteria? He ran to the church leaving her dripping on the Axminster and swooning in his chair. With great trepidation, he pushed open the door and entered the church. All was as it should be apart from the mess of flowers on the floor. There was no devil, no ghost. He stood in the silence scratching his head. He paced up and down the aisles, stopping to listen. Nothing, just the sound of his breathing and the tap of his shoes on the hard, stone floor.

༄

The following Sunday his congregation had swelled from the usual six to at least sixty six. Trevor couldn't understand it. He recognised some of the people, but most of them were complete strangers. It was most odd. But even odder was the fact that Mrs. Baker was missing.
   Then as his eyes perused the worshipers, the penny dropped. Word must have got out that Mrs Baker had encountered the devil in the church. Trevor noticed a man holding a tape recorder and another with a video camera. Well, well!
   After the service as the last of the congregation had left, the over-flowing collection plate had been transferred to a velvet bag and

Trevor was just locking the door when a group of people gathered around him.

'We're interested in the paranormal phenomena recently experienced in the church.' Their spokesman was an affable looking man in a green anorak and the remains of his breakfast was still in his beard. 'Would you mind if we investigated it?'

'In what way?' Trevor wasn't sure what to do. This was a first.

'We wouldn't disturb anything. We just want to set up our equipment and sit quietly.'

'Of course, yes, err, yes... you want to do this now?' Trevor's mind was in over-drive.

'That's what we had in mind, if it's convenient. My name is Kevin and this is my team.' Trevor turned to the group. A mixture of ages, about nine of them...yes nine, five men and four persons who could have been women, he wasn't sure. They looked harmless enough. 'We do need to raise money, the steeple... slowly crumbling I'm afraid, perhaps a small donation.' Trevor fingered the bag full of the day's collection.

'Sure, no problem.' Kevin extracted a fiver from each of his team and handed them over. 'Very generous, indeed,' Trevor stuttered, as he unlocked the church door. 'Would you like some refreshments- tea or coffee?'

꙳

Later as he handed out tea and the few Hobnobs Mrs Baker had left, he mentally reminded himself to replace the biscuits out of the forty-five pounds. Heck, he felt so flush he might even stretch to chocolate Hobnobs. This all went down well. Trevor left the little group in the church huddled around a monitor, making notes, and checking something called residual energy.

꙳

A few days later, Kevin pounded on the vicar's knocker in a state of extreme excitement. 'We had quite a productive night. Would you like to see what happened?' he gasped as he pushed past Trevor.

How could he refuse? Pulling his cassock over his knees, he settled himself down between Kevin and Kelly and peered at a laptop screen showing the interior of his church, and hoped he didn't have to watch hours and hours of it.

'We got some brilliant orbs,' Kevin said, 'and noises. There is definitely some unexplained phenomena.' All Trevor could see was empty pews and the dark patch where Mrs. Wilmot's boy had wet himself on the kneeling cushion.

'Now,' Kevin pointed to a speck of dust floating past the window. 'there's an orb.' Trevor didn't know what to say. He thought about the forty-five pounds donation and summoned up some enthusiasm. 'Extraordinary,' he said.

'There's another one, see how it changed direction.' Trevor squinted, it looked like a fly with the rays of the evening sun creating a halo effect around it. 'Yes, yes, extraordinary,' he added again, wondering how many more hours worth of dust and insects he was in for.

'There were noises too.' Kevin pulled out the tape recorder and switched it on, fast-forwarded the tape and stopped. There was the sound of static. He fast-forwarded it again until he came to a low rumbling noise. 'We were sitting quietly; this noise came from over there.'

Trevor listened. There were definite noises, a few muffled thumps and rustling. 'Extraordinary,' he said again.

'A very interesting evening.' Kevin said, 'Thank you so much for allowing us into your church.' 'Not at all, not at all,' Trevor repeated. He was pleased they were happy with the results. It seemed to Trevor it didn't take much to convince these people that ghosts walked the earth. And who was he to disillusion them; apart from the Holy Ghost, of course.

☙

Mrs Baker had been convinced. So convinced, she had not set foot in the church since the day of her fright, and it seemed there was nothing he could do to bring her back. The flower arrangements had deteriorated considerably since Mrs. Allsop had been roped in to do them. She seemed to think God's colours weren't enough and glitter sprayed everything. The church was beginning to look like a disco.

~

Trevor had often thought that writing sermons was a brilliant cure for insomnia. He was snoozing over his latest sermon when the telephone jolted him awake.

'My name is Tony Banks from Time Scale TV - can I speak to the Reverend Trevor Palmer?'

'Speaking,' Trevor said, wondering what Time Scale TV could possibly want to speak to him for.

'We would like to come and do a programme about the haunting.' Trevor was about to ask 'What haunting?' and stopped himself just in time. He answered with a long drawn out 'Yeeeessss.' Then Tony Banks said the magic words. 'We will pay you.'

'Ah, we do have a problem with the steeple and would appreciate a….'

'How much to fix the steeple?' Trevor's mind was racing. What would be a good figure? 'Errr, about one to two thousand pounds is what we're aiming for.'

'Great,' said Tony, 'Two thousand pounds is about the right ball park figure. I'll clear it with my producer. When would it be convenient to do the investigation?'

'As soon as possible,' Trevor replied, kicking himself for not aiming higher in the price stakes or asking to do the *'Pause for Thought'* slot on morning radio.

Everything was arranged. A whole team of professional Paranormal Investigators and film crew would arrive in two days. The church steeple fund would be two thousand pounds richer.

~

Trevor was getting used to supplying coffee and biscuits to ghost busters. As he brought them coffee the following morning, they looked somewhat dishevelled after their long night's vigil.

'How did it go?' he asked. 'Any spectres, orbs or anomalies?' He was also getting very knowledgeable about ghost busting jargon.

'Some interesting stuff.' Tony told him. 'Heard sounds, and felt a few cold spots. Won't know for sure until we've analysed the tapes.'

※

By Friday it had been three weeks since he'd seen Mrs Baker. She had stubbornly refused to see him. Probably thought he was the devil too, Trevor thought as he rang her door bell. He was greeted by a sour faced Mrs Baker.

'I'll not set foot in that church for as long as I live. The devil is within.' Mrs Baker came from a theatrical family. Her Uncle Silas' one man show of *'Madame Butterfly'* was still referred to in higher circles.

Trevor was about to utter, 'You silly woman,' when he stopped himself just in time. 'There is no devil in my church… in *God's church* Mrs. Baker. There has to be an explanation for the sound you heard. Don't let that one moment change your faith in our Saviour.'

'I'll not go in there,' she said crossing her arms over her chest like a shield.

'What if I go with you and stay until you've arranged the flowers, so I and the good Lord will watch over you?' Then he appealed to her vanity. 'No one can create floral arrangements as wonderful as yours Mrs Baker, you are *an artist.* You have a God-given gift.'

After what seemed like hours, Trevor miraculously persuaded Mrs Baker to accompany him into the church and under his watchful eye she swiftly set about arranging the flowers. A little more haphazardly than her usual way of working, but anything was better than the tinsel-infested petunia display that was Mrs Allsop's latest creation. He did feel a selfish sense of relief as Mrs Allsop's display was ruthlessly dismantled.

Trevor sat in the front pew and pondered the scriptures as Mrs Baker rushed about throwing long-stemmed blooms into unsuitably short vases and short-stemmed blooms into tall ones. Her hands trembled so violently that petals fell like rain.

Just as she was setting down a valiant display of the most exotic blooms on the north transept window sill, a bloodcurdling scream rent the air. A second scream even more bloodcurdling than the first issued from Mrs. Baker's throat. There was an almighty crash as the vase slipped from her fingers and a long moaning gurgle as she bolted for the door.

'Not another vase,' Trevor thought as he jumped from his pew. The scream repeated itself inside his head over and over. It seemed to have come from the little side chapel. He wandered over, checking walls, feeling for gaps, or openings. After two sets of ghost hunters, and sitting through several hours of tapes, Trevor was even more convinced now that there were no ghosts in his church, apart from the Holy Ghost.

He found himself in the little alcove under the stairs and thought he heard a rustle. He stood silent, listening. Another movement. It seemed to come from beneath his feet. He stamped down hard and a heart-wrenching scream went echoing round the walls. Like a flash he was down on his knees listening and tapping the floor; part stone, part wood. He felt an edge, his fingers traced it. A loose board, he squeezed his fingers under the edge and heaved with all his might. A hundred years of dust fell away.

He was peering into a cellar. A narrow beam of light slanted in from a broken air brick in the north wall. The smell was terrible. He began to think Mrs Baker was right and the devil did indeed dwell in this black hole beneath his church.

He saw a dead crow, its stomach ripped out, the remains of a rat, and what looked like the bushy tail of a squirrel with no body attached.

Then suddenly he was staring into the devil's eyes. They were green and mesmerising. For a second his heart missed a beat. Then the devil opened its mouth to reveal sharp pointed teeth and wailed.

'Oh, My God,' he took the Lord's name in vain. Then gasped. 'A cat! Mrs Baker's devil is a cat!'

୨

A little later back at the vicarage, Trevor watched as the half-starved, mangy moggy lapped milk from a saucer. This cat had earned two thousand and forty-five pounds towards the steeple fund, plus an eighty percent raise in the Sunday takings.

Mrs Baker would probably be on the phone at this moment, spreading the word. He could see it in his mind's eye. News teams, reporters, more ghost hunters, fame. Is this what he wanted?

The cat finished its milk and looked up at Trevor with what appeared to be an angelic expression.

Trevor smiled. His mind was made up.

God works in mysterious ways.
And the church did need
A new steeple.

Sandra Johnson
Crossed Lines

Linda couldn't shake the feeling of doom hanging over her. Something was wrong, she had felt it all day. And now sitting at her desk, staring at Year 8, who appeared to be working - a miracle in itself, the feeling still would not go away.

She had learnt over the years to trust her intuition. There was that time she obeyed the urge to go into the dining room, only to find a glass globe on the window sill had magnified the sunlight and set fire to a stack of exam papers. And that other time, she had had the urge to look in on her toddler as he slept, and found him dangling upside down with his foot stuck in a drawer.

So what could be wrong? Was it mum?

During afternoon break Linda rang her mother. The engaged tone rang in her ear. She must be alright, she thought, if she's talking on the phone. But just to be sure, fifteen minutes later she pressed redial. It was still engaged. Just before going back into Year 8 Design and Media Studies she rang again. By then her mother's telephone had been engaged for almost half an hour.

With trembling fingers Linda tapped in her sister Debbie's number. Not that she expected any help from that direction. Debbie's first priority was her pub, followed by her three dogs, two goldfish, a guinea pig called Harold and then Colin her husband who came last in the pecking order. Debbie answered on the fifth ring.

'Can you go round and check up on mum, I think something's wrong. Her phone's been off the hook for half an hour.'

'Sorry, no can do, up to my armpits in beer glasses and scampi. Abbi's not here and I'm holding the fort.'

'But she might be lying dead in a pool of blood.' Linda tried to lay it on at bit, but hell, it could be true.

'Then she won't need my help then will she?'

Linda gasped. She couldn't believe the callousness of her much unloved sister.

'I have a job too you know, and it's just as important as yours. Why do you always leave everything to me?'

'Oh listen to you. You always were such a good little girl.' Debbie sneered.

'Then keep ringing her just in case she is actually speaking to someone, and let me know if she answers. I can't make calls from the classroom.'

With that she shoved her phone into her pocket and headed back to Year 8, who weren't sitting comfortably. After calming them down, she then tried unsuccessfully to calm herself down. Her phone stayed ominously silent throughout the afternoon.

Finally, she could stand it no longer. Getting someone to sit with her year 8 class, she left the lesson and tried to phone her mother one last time. Still engaged! In seconds her boots were pounding along the corridor so hard little puffs of dust rose with each footfall. The cold air stung her lungs as she raced across the green to the car park. Without checking her mirrors or signalling, she manoeuvred out of the school gates, breaking the speed limit all the way to her mother's house.

Abandoning her car at an angle at her mother's gate, she dived up the path and pushed open the back door. Her mother never locked it. She could be murdered in her bed. Hell, she could be lying murdered in her bed right now. Suddenly Linda stopped dead. Chaos met her eyes. The kitchen was like a war zone. Scrambled egg was plastered on the ceiling, walls and floor. A bucket of water stood leaking a dark pool over the tiles, like blood. A mop lay where it had fallen beside it. The murder weapon. 'Arrrrhhhhh!' she screamed hurrying past the mess towards the living room.

For a second Linda surveyed the scene before her, reeling in the doorway, her head going dizzy with shock. Her mother was lying dead on the sofa with the radio roaring out *'Mull of Kintyre'*, to mask the sounds of her dying gasps, Linda thought.

Then the corpse moved, opened her eyes, sat up and smiled.

'Hello love, what are you doing here?'

'Oh my goodness, mother, you frightened me to death. What happened? I've been ringing you for hours.'

Her mother looked puzzled for a moment, then as if a light switched on in her brain said: 'Oh that, sorry I took the phone off the hook.'

'This is it,' thought Linda, 'She's past the post. Her mind's gone completely.' She was going to have to be locked up for her own protection.

'What made you take the phone off the hook? I've been ringing, Debbie's been ringing. We've been worried sick.' Well she could vouch for herself, she couldn't vouch for Debbie. 'And what happened in the kitchen? There's egg everywhere'

'Oh that.' Her mother smiled to herself, she looked quite sane, considering she was thinking about something quite as insane as chucky egg wall paper. 'I thought I'd make some scrambled egg for lunch. The eggs were from Mrs Farmer's hens, lovely they are, better than the ones from the supermarket.'

'Mother, I don't want to know who laid the eggs, I want to find out how they became plastered all over the kitchen.'

'I microwaved them. I always microwave eggs, they turn out lovely all soft and fluffy with no messy egg stuck to the pan. Makes it so easy to clean up afterwards.' Linda sighed and sank into the chair opposite her mother. This was going to be another of her mother's long-drawn-out explanations. 'I put them in for two minutes, just the same as I did them yesterday. I usually mash them with a fork because they come out in one lump, don't they? Well that's when it happened.'

'What mother? What happened?'

'I'm trying to tell you aren't I? Don't interrupt. You always were impatient. As I was saying the minute I stuck the fork in to mash them, it all exploded. Gave me a right shock it did. There must have been something funny about those eggs. They went everywhere.'

'I know they went everywhere. I've just walked in through the kitchen.'

'Yes, well you didn't see it. It was in my hair, in my ears, up my nose...'

'Okay mother I get the picture. So what has an exploding egg got to do with taking the phone off the hook?'

'I was coming to that. Don't fluster me. I had to clean the egg off myself didn't I? I was upstairs changing my clothes when the phone rang. I was standing there in my underwear with the phone going like the clappers. I had to answer it in my vest and knickers.' Linda sank even deeper into the chair. 'It was only a stupid Scottish man asking if I rented my telephone from BT. So I told him if he didn't know that, I wasn't going to tell him. Then I went back upstairs and was combing the egg out of my hair when the phone rang again. I thought it might be important. It could have been you checking to see if I was behaving myself.'

'And?' Linda was losing the will to live.

'It was a very nice man offering to fit a new kitchen free of charge.'

Linda nearly jumped out of the seat. 'Mother, you haven't ordered a kitchen?'

'No, of course not. Do I look like I was born yesterday? I told him I'd love a new kitchen and then gave him Dorothy Miller's address.'

'You did WHAT?'

'Never mind that, I'm trying to explain. I was still in my knickers and vest and my hair was all over the place...'

'Mother can we skip this bit and get to the part where you are decent again, and taking the phone off the hook.'

'You are impatient; it's bad for your heart you know. Stress!'

Linda heaved a huge sigh, didn't she know it.

'So I had to clean the kitchen, you should have seen the mess.'

'I did mother. I saw the mess. The mess is still there.'

'That's because I was halfway through mopping the floor when the phone rang again.'

'Who was it this time?'

'I don't know, with the mop bucket in the way, and the floor all wet, and me trying to step over the bit of floor I'd cleaned, by the time I got to the phone they'd hung up. It was then that I noticed the time. Five past two. Time for the *'Afternoon Play'* on the wireless.'

'Mother, it hasn't been called a wireless for fifty years. It's called a radio now.'

'I know it's called a radio. My short term memory has gone, and wireless is the first word that pops into my head, not radio. Anyway that's got nothing to do with the explanation. Do you want me to finish telling you?'

'Yes mother, I'm sorry, go on, I'm listening,' she sighed.

'Well as I was saying it was five past two, I'd missed the beginning of the *'Afternoon Play'* and I was just going to switch on the wir….radio, when the bloody phone rang again. By this time I'd had enough, well you would wouldn't you? I don't know why I answered it really, but I did.'

'Who was it?' It was like trying to nail semolina to a wall. Linda waited.

'A strange man. He asked me where I got my power from. Well I told you I'd had enough didn't I? So I said - I get my power from *Kryptonite* - now bugger off. So I put the phone down before it had a chance to ring again and I left it off the hook. Then I put my feet up to listen to the *'Afternoon Play'* in peace and quiet, only it must have been really boring because I couldn't keep my eyes open. Must have fallen asleep. And that's when you came in and woke me up.'

Linda gave her mother a relieved smile. She hadn't gone doolally yet, well no more doolally than she'd always been. She stood up, gave her mother a hug, and said, 'I'll go and put the kettle on.'

'While you're at it could you just wipe that bit of egg off the wall.' Her mother grinned. 'And run the mop over that little bit of floor I missed.'

As Linda headed out to the kitchen she caught her mother's whispered words.

'You always were such a good little girl.'

Sandra Johnson
The Gift

The old tramp was there again. As Emma approached, her expression softened. He was sitting upright, feet together and shoulders straight. He must have been a military man, Emma had first thought. She wondered how such a dignified, disciplined man could have ended up like this, helpless and in dirty clothes. He wore a tie, even though his shirt collar was so frayed it was almost detached from the shirt. His trousers were too big for his old body and hung over his feet. He was in his usual position staring straight ahead at the autumn trees, yet his eyes seemed unfocused, pale-rimmed and cloudy.

Emma had felt sorry for him the first day she had passed by. That was Monday. All the way home she had scolded herself for not offering him some money. This she was able to rectify, because on her way home the following day he was still there on the same bench in the same pose, the same unfocused stare, a tattered and torn rucksack at his side. Emma had stopped and said hello as she delved into her bag, searching for her purse. He had turned to look at her, had accepted the two pounds, gazed at it in his upturned palms, nodded serenely and in a surprisingly educated accent had thanked Emma profusely for her kindness. Smiling to herself as she went on her way, Emma had felt good. She was glad she had had the opportunity to help the tramp after all.

On the third day, Emma had given him a sandwich and a Kit Kat, and on the fourth day she had stopped at a bakery and bought him a hot pasty and a cup of coffee. Each time he had thanked her over and over again, as if he had been given gold or diamonds and not just a bite to eat.

And here he was again, on the same park bench, in the same shabby clothes, the same crinkly, grey beard covering most of his face. Emma had been thinking of the tramp all day, wondering if he would still be there and what she should do. Could she afford to give him money or food every day? It seemed difficult to stop now that she'd started, but amazingly it gave her so much pleasure. She began to think what lovely gift she could give him today. The bakery made delicious quiches, spicy sausage rolls, every type of pie you could think of. She chose a hot steak and kidney pie and a polystyrene cup of carrot and coriander soup, then hurried through the park - she didn't want the food to get cold. He'll really enjoy this, she thought as she headed along the familiar path.

And there he was in his usual place, only today he was peering down the path in her direction looking for her. His eyesight wasn't too good because she was almost by his side before he recognised her.

'I was hoping you would come,' he said, looking really pleased. 'I've got something for you.'

Emma sat down beside him, the tray of food on her lap. She watched as the tramp rummaged through his tattered canvas bag. He pulled out a rusty, dented biscuit tin, the Coronation of Queen Elizabeth showing through the scratches. He had attempted to make it look like a gift by wrapping a frayed piece of tartan ribbon around it, and securing it with a knot.

'Are you sure?" Emma asked, "I really couldn't take it. It looks too precious.'

The tramp pushed the tin towards her, and in his educated voice said. 'My dear, I really want you to have this. Please take it. You'll make an old man happy.'

Emma took the tin, and passed the little cardboard tray to the tramp. 'And I want you to have this,' she said, 'before it gets cold.'
The tramp's face lit up as he removed the lid from the soup. Emma watched as he sipped, her hands clutching the tin he had given her. She wondered what was in it. It felt empty. Even if it was empty, it was a lovely gift. To be given something by someone who had nothing seemed more precious than an expensive gift from a rich person, and the tin in itself was precious, it was almost an antique.

'Open it,' the tramp said, between mouthfuls of steak and kidney pie. He had spread a paper napkin over his lap as if he were dining at the Ritz.

Emma looked at the tin, then carefully began undoing the knotted ribbon. She then prized the lid up off the box. It was almost empty. There were just three photos inside. The top one was bent and scratched. She picked it up and peered at it.

'It's beautiful, ' she said. 'Where is it?'

'I used to live there.. Longhurst Hall. Have you heard of it?'

'No,' Emma replied. 'Did you work there?'

'No, my dear, it was my house, I owned it. A wonderful place, in Berkshire you know. Became a bit too much for us, gave it to the National Trust.'

'Gosh!' Emma was dumbfounded.

'Bought a little house in Hertfordshire.'

Emma picked up the next photograph, a little square of black and white. Only you wouldn't call the house in the photo little. She counted eight windows on the second floor.

'Is this the house you bought?'

'Yes, Ashton House. We were very happy there.'

Emma noticed a tear in the tramp's eye. She sat silently, waiting. She picked up the last photo. It was a man and a woman and a little girl. She looked at it for ages, not knowing what to say. The woman was pretty, and the man was handsome. He was holding out a large fish which he must have caught and he was smiling proudly.

The tramp began to speak quietly. 'Yes we were all happy there, lived there for thirty years. That's my wife Maud, and our daughter Emily. All dead now. Emily look so much like you, she had the same kind eyes.'

'I'm so sorry.' Emma wanted to stroke this poor man's hand. He had finished his soup and had eaten his pie, and was looking at Emma with the kindest eyes.

'She was so ill, my Emily. At least Maud was spared seeing her suffer. Don't be sad dear,' he said, 'I'll be joining them soon. I have no more family, and had no one to leave Ashton House to. But now I have.'

Emma didn't have a clue what he meant. Was he saying he still owned the house in the photo? But he was an old tramp. She looked at him and frowned.

'I would like you to have our house. We were so happy there, and I want you to live there and be happy.'

'B-b-but, Emma stammered. 'I don't understand. Why aren't you living there? Why do you look like you have nowhere to go? '

'Ah! There are so few really good people in this world don't you think? I like to think I've been fishing for one.'

Emma blinked at him.

'You know dear, fishing! Only instead of silk fly, I used these clothes.' He stretched out his legs. For the first time Emma could see the tips of his shoes pointing out from under the filthy trousers. Handmade Italian leather.

'I'm sorry to have tricked you my dear, but, I did enjoy the little feasts you brought me.'

Emma looked back down at the photo of the smiling family.

'You will be happy there for a long time too I think dear. I'm just very lucky to have found you before the winter comes.'

Emma could think of nothing to say. She hugged the tin to her and together they sat in silence, and watched the golden leaves drift to the earth like feathers from the wings of angels.

Trevor K. Bell
A Forest Tale

Although it has been said that emotion is the enemy of reason, it seems to me that emotion is there *for* a reason - at least I have found it to be true - and people ignore it at their peril. If it *is* a truth, it is one Mr Filac ignored as he set out that unfortunate day into the forest to locate his tormentor. I imagine, on that occasion, his feelings were rather like ours. We are often not sure why we are embarking on a certain course of action, are filled, even, with a certain sense of foreboding, yet persist in it all the same. But I am not a philosopher; this is how it happened:-

In 1799 Mr Filac inherited the remnant of an estate; namely, an isolated farmhouse and its adjoining forest of several thousand acres, formerly the property of his uncle, declared deceased. It was a farmhouse of moderate size built of rough-hewn stone blocks - as are many in the Aveyron–Auvergne Districts of France - with narrow windows set deeply into its walls. To the north of the farmhouse a track ran several miles through the forest to a minor road; from thence, a few more miles to a hamlet. The corners of the building were defended by large jutting stones as if the builder knew, even at the time of its construction, that it would have to withstand some sort of an assault. A shuttered extension ran along the whole of the west side of the property, while underneath, in the south-west corner, was a place where his uncle had kept (although they were never shown to anyone) creatures he had brought back from the African subcontinent. One of these, according to the *Journal Francais* - was a large bi-pedal creature, with large breasts and, according to some witnesses, shockingly thick red hair. Apparently, it was kept with a dark-haired, quite different, smaller companion which appeared almost human.   Little else is known about them.   For instance, there is no mention of their species, habits or nature, or their specific habitat in Africa, or from where they were taken.

The farmhouse was set on a hill; or, rather, on a calcareous plateau surrounded by ancient forests of oak, beech and fir. His uncle had cleared the forest to two-hundred metres all around the house, giving rise to the speculation that the clearance had been done to give early warning of whatever might come out of the forest. In all honesty, we do not know if the forest had been cleared before the arrival of the creatures, or afterwards, only that at some point, the larger creature escaped and there was speculation that his uncle had gone in search of it.   As his uncle had disappeared about this time, it seemed a reasonable deduction.

☙

It was known that Mr Filac, who had lived alone in *Marseilles* for many years, initially, greatly enjoyed the solitude afforded by its location, particularly as it enabled him to pursue his keen interest in astronomy. The splendidly dark skies around the Aveyron farmhouse made the stars shine far brighter in his sky than in the light-polluted canopy of Marseilles. In particular, the Dog Star Sirius, was thrillingly bright and Orion's hunting dog provided dazzling company for the greater part of the year. He also had with him his earthly dog, Pascal, a half-mad King Charles spaniel – which was not a hunting dog.

Unfortunately, not long after taking up residence, Mr Filac's nocturnal idyll was disrupted by a fearful sound emanating from the forest. According to those who heard it (if description could, indeed, be applied to it) it was something between a roar and a howl; similar to, but quite unlike the sound made by any known forest creature. It could be heard, faintly, as far away as the closest distant hamlet referred to earlier. There, the local priest, Father Drebonet, interviewed by the *gendarmerie* after Mr Filac's disappearance, thought it was like an anguished wailing ('as if from the pit of hell itself,' as he put it) for no more horrifying a sound, in his opinion, could possibly have emanated from anywhere else.

The fearful noise began to affect Mr Filac's nerves. We know from his diary, he was traumatised by nightmares and, once or twice, whether asleep or awake, eyes open or shut (he could not tell), he fancied he saw a large, bi-pedal creature, russet in colour, with a shaggy mane and short thick horns, which latter detail, of course, when reported in the nearby hamlet, gave credence to Father Drebonet's belief that the creature *was* from the Devil. On some nights, when he heard the roar close to the house, he jumped out of bed and ran and locked himself in a small room at the end of the corridor, where he remained until dawn. On one occasion, he reached out to close a window, and felt something powerful and coarse-haired, brush against his arm. Thereafter, all doors and windows were securely locked well before dark, and Pascal was stationed at the front door to stand guard. Several times he sent for the priest, as he began to entertain the belief that the creature was, as Father Drebonet claimed, 'not of this world'. Unfortunately, nothing would persuade Father Drebonet to set foot in the forest - day or night, and Mr Filac was, effectively, abandoned.

He was relieved when a local hunter called at the farmhouse, selling game, as it provided him with an opportunity to make enquiries.

'*Bonjour Monsieur, que voudriez vous une lapin, bebe cochon?*', the hunter asked, hoisting several creatures aloft on a wooden pole, a large grin spreading across his face. Mr Filac pointed to a carcass, indicating that he would have the rabbit but not the young piglet. The hunter passed the carcass to Mr Filac, who hung its rigid, lifeless, body on a hook behind the door, out of Pascal's reach.

'You have hunted in this part of the forest a long time?' asked Mr Filac.

'*Oui Monsieur*', replied the hunter, as he fumbled in his pocket for the exchange money for the rabbit.

'Everyone is talking about Father Drebonet's demon in the forest?'

Pascal began to bark for the rabbit.

'Ah! One can always hear and see things in the forest; it is always playing tricks' said the hunter. 'There is a story of a forest creature which haunts this part of the forest. The priest believes it; but the truth – who knows?' He shrugged his shoulders and walked briskly off in the opposite direction to which he had come.

Disappointed, but undeterred, the next day Mr Filac took the long journey to Clemont-Ferrard, where he intended to acquaint himself with the natural history of the region. He thought to research the identity of the creature. He arrived In the town and, after a *potee avergnate* in the *place de jaude*, he was pleased to find a booksellers and discovered a book on the natural history of the area, revealing that a surprising variety of predatory animals had once lived in the forest, particularly during the Graveltian and Early Magdalenian period (Mr Filac was something of a palaeontologist) including lions, panthers, bears and hyenas. Evidence of their existence was plentiful, in the form of cave-drawings and paintings, [1] but he could find nothing remotely matching the fearful creature of his nightmares.

'You are looking to identify the type of forest creature that everyone in the district is talking about?' asked the bookseller.

'Yes', said Mr Filac, brightening.

'It is a fable, a forest phantom', he said, and he walked over to the section of the bookshelves which dealt with myths, fables, and legends: 'You may find something here'.

But after leafing through the collection, and reading those that looked most promising, Mr Filac came up empty handed and began his journey homeward.

Unfortunately, he had misjudged the return journey time, a mist had descended, and it began to grow dark. Just two miles from the farmhouse, where the track passed through an avenue of trees, his horse suddenly reared up and refused his command to move forward. Next, he heard the sound of something powerful rushing towards his position, through the trees. Immediately, a picture of the forest creature flashed into his mind and he began to panic. Just behind him the creature emerged from the forest and made the fearful sound with which he had become so familiar. In the next instant, the horse reared up, and then shot forward. After a ferocious gallop, and without glancing behind him for fear of what he might see, he

---

[1] *A not dissimilar collection of paintings may be seen today in the Chavvet Cave, located in the commune of Vallon –Pont-d'Arc, above the former bed of the Ardeche River.*

reached the farmhouse, abandoned the horse and rushed inside, bolting the door. He ran up to his bedchamber, where he sat, in the dark, hardly daring to breathe, his senses on high alert, watching and listening to the sounds of the forest but nothing further occurred and two hours later he retired.

Before he fell asleep, he was inclined to leave the farmhouse for good. But by the morning, he had changed his mind and decided he would take a gun and kill the creature. And so, a few days later, he started making his preparations and took nightly compass bearings to determine the creature's general location.

A few days before departure, he discovered in an old chiffonier, a journal written in his uncle's hand, clearly indicating that his deceased uncle had made his own expedition. Furthermore, in the back of the same diary, carefully folded was an article cut out of a newspaper, dated 1798, describing the famous discovery of a naked boy of eleven or twelve years of age, found alone near Mr Filac's part of the forest. Of course, it was the true account of the discovery of the 'Wild Boy' of Aveyron; a male child, subsequently given the name Jean-Piere Cargol, who had been wholly conditioned by his forest environment, and found to be completely lacking in human language and social understanding. The doctor, he read, who had examined the boy, a Dr Jean Itard, was unable to explain how the child had come to be wild in the forest in the first place, or, indeed, how he could have been nurtured without a lactating mother. This caused speculation that the child might have been raised by escaped monkeys; in particular, by a lactating female who, perhaps, having lost her own offspring had sought to satisfy her maternal instincts by 'adopting' the boy. Yet another suggestion was that the boy had been suckled by a she-wolf (in the Florentine 'Romulus and Remus' tradition). The theories were advanced for lack of better ones. As everyone knows, the baffling case of Jean-Piere Cargol was never fully explained and remains a mystery to this day.[2]

With the article still fresh in his mind, Mr Filac completed his expeditionary preparations and set off, accompanied by Pascal, one

---

[2] *This true, famous, account of the discovery of the Wild Boy of Aveyron is readily available in several publications.*

hot sultry day. As they pushed through the forest, he had the distinct feeling that he was being followed; several times he span round, almost expecting to see the nightmare creature behind him, but saw nothing. The feeling persisted until, after several miles, they made an overnight camp which, apart from being plagued by swarms of flies, passed without incident. The next day they journeyed for several hours until they came to the top of a river bluff, which looked down on fast-flowing water in the gorge below. He was disappointed to find there was no way over the river bluff, and he would have to descend into the gorge if he wished to directly follow the compass bearing he had chosen.

Reluctant to abandon his search, Mr Filac buttoned Pascal into his jacket and they began to climb down into the gorge. It was a dizzying undertaking, and several times he almost missed his foothold, losing the rifle and sending rocks crashing down into the river until, in darkening light, they reached a precipitous ledge fifty yards above the river. Again, he was disappointed to find there was no way forward around the bluff. Resignedly, he unfastened Pascal and put him down on the ledge, shortly intending to retrace his steps.

However, after a few minutes rest, he noticed a small opening in the cliff face further along the ledge and he made his way precariously towards it, the whimpering Pascal, following. He slid past a bush and through a narrow opening. To his surprise, he found himself in a large chamber whose recesses ended in darkness. Immediately he was taken aback by the shocking, pungent, smell of an animal. 'Good God, what's this!?' he said to himself, amazed at what he had found. However, try as he might, he could not persuade Pascal to enter the cave, who remained whimpering outside.

Lighting his torch, which he had carefully remembered to bring with him, he saw, to his left, a pile of twigs and branches forming a kind of rude nest - not unlike those made by the great apes of Africa; while, to his right, scattered over the floor, were piles of white and grey bones, some of great age, others were much younger. Here and there, he was horrified to see scraps of flesh, fur and shattered skulls. Clearly, the cave was inhabited by a powerful carnivore. Its walls were decorated with paintings of predatory animals - the lions, panthers, bears and rhinos he had read about in Clemont-Ferrard. There was a chimerical figure in ochre red which, above the waist, was similar in form to the upper body of a woman, its horns and hooves contrasted in black magnesium resembling in part the creature of his nightmares. Imprinted in the clay floor of the cave, he was astonished to see a child's footprints. Then, to his right, two skeletons were slumped against a wall, seemingly embracing one another in mutual companionship; one seemed that of a small child, and the other- who knew what? Mr Filac became very excited – as excited as he had ever been - and he walked into a pool of water, so clear, that he did so without realising.

Suddenly, outside, Pascal began to bark loudly, and then, in the next instant, to whimper. There was a loud painful yelp, and nothing further was heard from him. It was then that Mr Filac heard the same fearful roar he had heard from the farmhouse; only this time, the sound was batted between the walls of the cave. He heard the creature push past the bush at the entrance to the cave. To his horror, he realised there was no prospect of escape, and, to make matters worse, he managed to drop the torch, extinguishing the flame. The creature's roar was repeated several times and, with a dreadful realization, he knew it was moving towards him in the darkness. Horribly soon, he felt the exhalation of its foul breath upon his face and, in the next instant, it lifted him vertically several feet off the ground. He felt, rather than saw, two pitiless eyes examining his own and heard the sound of its powerful jaws opening. A bead of saliva fell from the creature's mouth onto his face.

Unsurprisingly, Mr Filac's remains were never found. Like his uncle, there was no corpse, and he was eventually declared, legally, deceased. His estate passed to his cousin who soon heard the same fearful roar emanating from the forest, and it was not long before he went in search of its owner.

Anne Abbinnett
Calling Time

Henry toiled up the hill to the viewpoint overlooking the river. Boxer, his old Labrador trailed behind, panting and limping along on his arthritic legs. It was a sad fact but age was catching up with both of them. Today was Henry's birthday and, although he loved flowers the brave display of daffodils in the park did nothing to lighten his mood.

At the top, he clung to the railings, his breath coming in harsh gasps. Boxer collapsed with a grateful sigh at his feet. Ever since they'd moved to the town so many decades ago, this view had always been a favourite with Henry and his wife, Sally. He stared down at the water; white caps skittered across the surface, whipped up by a stiff breeze. Apart from a lone ferry chugging its way from Birkenhead to Liverpool the river was empty. He could remember when the Mersey had been a busy, bustling place, bristling with boats and ships of all shapes and sizes from all over the world. But the world had been a different place then. He and Sally had been full of hope, their whole life before them, the day they'd first stood on this spot- how long ago? Henry couldn't remember. Time had ceased to mean very much since Sally had died. The only thing he was absolutely sure about, was how old he was.

He looked at his hands clenched round the railings; practical hands Sally had called them, square and capable. Not that they were much use now. Knobbly and gnarled with rheumatism, they could hardly hold a knife and fork never mind a screwdriver.

He turned away and slumped down on a nearby bench, wincing as the bones of his thin frame met the hard wood. Boxer opened one eye, decided Henry wasn't going to move and closed it again. Henry sighed. He hadn't expected to feel so bereft at Sally's death - two years ago was it? They'd talked about it, one of them dying, even made plans, how they would get on with the rest of their lives, keep doing the things they enjoyed, seeing friends, going on holiday. But after all the discussions and the planning, he hadn't been prepared when it happened. Life ceased to hold the same attraction than when he'd shared it with Sally.

He was roused from despondency by the shouts of two small children racing towards him in hot pursuit of a flop-eared mongrel. Henry watched their attempts to catch hold of the pup with amusement. He was reminded of his own children when they were small and the fun they'd had with that long-eared gangly pup they'd loved. Boxer, the last in a long line of such dogs, was roused from his snooze and struggled to sit up alarmed by the young dog's antics. It bounded and pranced around barking, clearly inviting the old dog to join in.

'Doesn't he want to play, mister?' the smaller child asked.

'He's a bit too old for play, son.' said Henry. 'Best not disturb him.'

Shouting, the children ran off down the path, the pup racing after them and everything was still again.

Henry shuffled forward on the bench. 'Come on Boxer, my old fellow, time to go. It's my birthday today you know. Did you know that? I'm eighty five today. We'd better go home and see what that daughter of mine has been up to. Getting a few friends in for tea she says. Lot of nonsense at my age.'

A long shaft of sunlight broke through the clouds. Henry squinted at the brightness, deepening the wrinkles round his eyes. Leaning heavily on his stick he pushed himself upright, stretching to ease the stiffness out of his legs and, patting the dog on its head they both started back down the hill.

Anne Abbinnett
Communication Breakdown

It had started to rain as Harriet knelt to place the bouquet of roses on her mother's grave. A misty, soaking rain that mingled with the tears that slid down her cheeks. She felt she'd lived a thousand lifetimes in the week since the funeral. Knowing that death had brought relief from constant pain did nothing to ease her grief. Her mother had always been there for her; without her loving presence Harriet had no idea how she was going to cope. Friends were well meaning and kind to a fault but they didn't or couldn't understand the bond that had existed between them.

Somewhere a phone was ringing. It took Harriet a few seconds to realise it was her mobile. With an impatient tug she pulled it out of her pocket and stared at the blank screen. The ringing persisted.

'No, no, not again,' she moaned. Flipping it open she barked, 'Yes.'

As before there was only static undulating up and down like waves on a shore. Harriet snapped the phone shut and burst into tears. That was the umpteenth time that had happened in the last two days. It really was too much to bear at the moment.

The assistant in the shop where she'd bought the mobile had just shrugged his shoulders and said, 'Who knows what's going on up there in the ether with so many lines of communication criss-crossing each other.' In spite of the rain Harriet decided to walk home, putting off the moment when she would have to brave the emptiness of the flat.

She heard the phone ringing as she put the key in the lock. Rushing in, she picked up the receiver. Static, ebbing and flowing. But, there *was* something. Something underneath. A voice? She couldn't be sure.

'Hello! Hello! Is someone there?...I'm sorry, I can`t hear you.' She paused. Under the static there was definitely a voice but so faint she couldn`t make sense of it.

'I`m sorry, I can`t hear you. Please, speak up.' Then silence, broken only by the sound of her ragged breath. With shaking hands Harriet replaced the receiver. This was getting ridiculous. Why was this happening now, when she most needed the telephones. Her head ached. Utterly weary now, unable to even think about eating, Harriet went to bed.

She woke from a deep troubled sleep. The phone was ringing. She blinked at the clock; 3.30. It took a while to register. Harriet sat bolt upright; no one rings at 3.30 in the morning unless something is badly wrong.

Racing through to the hall she grabbed the receiver yelling, 'Yes. I`m here. What`s happened? Who is it?' White noise. Static rising and falling like children on a see-saw. Harriet gripped the receiver, whispering, 'Who are you? What do you want?' A voice, faint as a shadow under the static. 'I can`t hear you. Say again. 'Move?' What do you mean - move?'

Silence. Then the dialling tone. Harriet replaced the receiver and stood, her body shaking with fear and bewilderment.

Over the next few days Harriet dealt with all the business that accumulates when a person dies. Too tired and weary with grief to cope with the erratic behaviour of the phones, she turned off her mobile and refused to answer the land-line unless someone left a message on the answer machine. At night she simply unplugged it.

Compassionate leave used up, Harriet had to return to work. She needed her job more than ever now. But the thought of having to face her colleagues and their condolences filled her with dread. All she wanted to do was curl up in a dark hole and wish the world away.

On the evening before her return to work, unable to concentrate Harriet flicked through the television channels, her mind filled with a million memories. Her attention was caught by a photo-fit picture of a man wanted, the programme presenter said, for rape and murder. She knew that face. How? Focused now, Harriet wondered why he seemed so familiar. It wasn't a distinctive face, quite ordinary really. But she had seen the person behind the face of that she was certain. Where? Was he a customer at the bank where she worked? She couldn't remember. Dismissing it as unimportant Harriet went into the kitchen to make a nightcap. In the living room the television twittered on, reminding people, young women in particular, to be very careful about opening their doors to strangers. A survivor of an attack had let the perpetrator into her flat on the pretext of borrowing some coffee.

The following day proved to be every bit as harrowing as Harriet had imagined. Colleagues were kind; they knew how close she'd been to her mother. The ones she appreciated the most simply hugged her and said nothing.

The time went slowly. And then her computer started playing up. The screen would suddenly go blank then come back with a load of gibberish. The firm's engineers couldn't find anything wrong and put the problem down to being idle for two weeks. But the problem only got worse. E-mails would appear with row upon row of unrelated letters and occasionally a single word 'move'. It became so bad that Harriet began to wonder if perhaps she was somehow responsible for making the surrounding technology malfunction. She shrugged the feeling away; this wasn't the time to get paranoid. But when she started getting e-mails with the words 'move away' printed over and over again, Harriet became seriously worried. What did it all mean? No one else was having problems with their machines. What was going on? Could she after all, because of her state of mind, be causing it?

Over the next few days the message 'move away now' became so frequent and urgent that Harriet was afraid to turn her computer on. One of the office wags laughingly suggested she was being haunted. Aghast, Harriet thought of her mum and burst into tears.

'Don't take any notice,' said best friend Cassie. 'The poor lad is obviously a sandwich short of a picnic. Look, what you need is a good night out. What do you say to a meal and stiff drink at the pub?'

It was, Harriet decided as she got ready, a very good idea. Just what she needed to get her life back to normal. Locking the door to the flat she turned to go downstairs and almost bumped into a dark figure standing behind her on the landing.

'I'm sorry,' a deep voice said, `did I startle you?'

As the man moved on up the stairs Harriet caught a glimpse of his face in the dim light. She froze. She`d seen him somewhere before. The photo-fit picture from the television popped into her mind. She thought she`d seen that man before too. Were they the same person? No, that was impossible. Just because they both seemed familiar and she couldn`t remember how she knew them, didn't mean they were the same person. Harriet shook her head, the strain of the last few weeks was beginning to affect her badly.

The front door burst open as Harriet went downstairs and Mrs Brewster from the ground floor flat bustled in. She hugged Harriet and said how very sorry she was about her mother and how was she bearing up. Harriet thanked the old lady for her concern and fought down the urge to blurt out all the problems she was having with phones and computers.

Instead, she said, 'By the way, have we a new tenant in the top flat?'

Mrs Brewster looked at her, frowning. 'Didn't you know dear. It was taken over two months ago.'

'No,' Harriet replied. 'I'm a bit out of touch I suppose what with mother and everything.'

'Of course you are. Understandable. He seems a pleasant young man. Never know he was there if you didn't want to, if you see what I mean.'

Harriet nodded. That explained how she knew him. Over the last two months she must have seen him and it simply hadn't registered.

In the pub Harriet felt a bit of the tension drift away. Cassie had been right, she needed to get some normality back into her life. Start seeing friends again. Perhaps the new tenant was worth getting to know. For the first time in many months she felt lighter and more at ease.

Harriet hummed a little tune as she opened the door to her flat. Inside felt cosy and warm; a safe refuge against the rest of the world. Still humming she switched on her computer to check for e-mails and the television to catch the news. But it was *'Crime Watch'* again; the wind-up after the news. The photo-fit picture flashed up onto the screen. Harriet regarded it, smiling at her own silliness. Yes, there was a fleeting resemblance to the new tenant, but that was all. Time for a nightcap and then bed. She went into the kitchen and switched on the kettle. The doorbell rang.

Harriet was about to open the door when the telephone started to ring. Calling out to whoever was on the other side of the door, 'Just a minute...' she picked up the phone.

Under the static a frantic voice; 'Don`t open,' it said, over and over.

Alarmed, Harriet peered through the peephole in the door. The man from upstairs was standing there, an empty coffee jar in his hand. Harriet gasped and backed away. Turning she caught a glimpse of the letters on the computer screen swirling round and round. Her eyes widened in horror as they formed themselves into a clear sentence. 'DANGER DON`T OPEN THE DOOR.' The static stopped and the telephone was silent. Then Harriet, paralysed with fright, could only stare open mouthed, as a favourite picture of her mother fell to the floor.

Anne Abbinnett
The Answer's in the Stars

Have you finished with the paper yet?

No, you can see I'm still reading it.

Will you be finished soon?

Don't know - it depends.

On what?

Whether I can maintain an interest. Is it important?

Well I would like a glimpse before going to work. Oh, just give me the middle section.

What's so important about the middle section? (pause) No don`t tell me it's the horoscopes isn't it?

(Sighs deeply) So! What's it to you?

Nothing. I`m just surprised you still believe in that rubbish.

I don`t believe it.

Then why bother reading them?

Well you never know do you.

Never know what?

There might be some truth in there somewhere.

That has got to be the most illogical thing I've ever heard you say.

I'm a woman, I'm allowed to be illogical.

That's true.

Anyway lots of famous people consult astrologers. Some say it's a science. That should appeal to your logical, reasonable outlook on life.

That's rubbish! Not my outlook but that it's called a science - and what 'sane' famous people read their horoscopes?

Ok. Let's see now. Mmm...Hitler, Ronald Reagan...(pause) Ah! I see what you mean.

I rest my case.

Are you going to give me the paper?

No.

Now you're being selfish.

No, I'm being logical and sensible for you.

But I don`t want your logic or your sense. I just want the paper.

Oh, alright. (Long pause) Well what does it say?

Do you really want to know? It's not too whimsical for you, too unscientific?

Go on, I`m big enough to bear it.

Well my stars say- 'After a contentious start your day will improve if you spend your time with more congenial companions.'

Huh! That could apply to anyone anywhere. (pause) What does mine say?

Are you ready for this? Right. It says-'Beware trying to impose your opinions on others, they will not appreciate it.'

I don`t believe you. You`re making it up. Give that paper to me.....oh! It`s still rubbish.

Anne Abbinnett
Homeless

It`s freezing
and I see you there,
every day,
a dog by your side
begging.
I hurry past,
busy,
noticing the card
'Homeless'
out of the corner of my eye.

Shuddering,
I try to imagine
being homeless,
but my life is comfortable,
secure,
I don`t have to worry
about food
or shelter.

It`s freezing
and I see you there,
every day.
I drop a coin
as I hurry by.
I want to know
why are you alone,
begging in the street,
but am afraid
to ask.

Anne Abbinnett

Leap of Faith

We were sitting in my kitchen drinking tea and chatting when Betty suddenly asked me what was wrong. I didn't know what she meant and said so.

'Well you seem a bit remote and not really like yourself at all.'

Betty has been my best friend for more years than I care to remember so I just had to blurt it all out didn't I. It had been building up for months and I was getting close to not being able to stand it any longer.

'I don't understand,' she said. 'You've been together for a very long time. Why now?'

I thought for a bit, chin on hand. 'I'm not sure really. It's because it *is* a long time I think. It didn't matter when Joe and I first met. We were living together until his divorce came through and then Polly was born, it just didn't seem relevant, until now. Now I want everything to be legal. *I* want to be legal.'

Betty was still puzzled. 'But why does it matter now, why now?'

I took another sip of tea. 'Betty I haven't got it all sorted out in my own mind yet. I think it's got something to do with my age and Joe's retirement coming up next year.'

Betty was frowning. It was obvious she still couldn't see why it was bothering me so much. 'Look Sheila, I know I've been married to Harry for over forty years but I've never given your unmarried state a second thought. I assumed you were rock solid. Well you are, aren't you?'

I could see doubt was beginning to colour her perception of the situation.

'You don't think Joe is, well...?'

I looked at her knowing exactly what she was hinting at. 'What do I think?'

'That Joe is playing away.' She paused looking distinctly unhappy. 'Do you?'

I laughed then. 'No, he's not playing away as you so quaintly put it. If there is one thing I'm sure of it's his faithfulness.'

'Then what's the problem? You say it's to do with age and retirement, but there's got to be more to it than that.'

If there was one positive thing about this conversation it was helping me get down to the real issues and I realised then what the nub of the problem was.

'Well yes, if I'm honest, there is. To other people I've always been Mrs Jones and I'm not entitled to be called Mrs. Then there's Joe's grandchildren, they call me Gran and I don't feel comfortable not being officially their grandmother. I feel as if I'm living a lie and it's becoming a burden.'

Betty sat silent for a long moment. 'I see. When you put it like that I do see what you mean. It's awkward isn`t it.'

And we sat, two friends silently sipping tea, caught in that quietness that speaks of long friendship and understanding.

Eventually Betty put her cup down and took hold of both my hands. 'If that's how you feel, Sheila, then we must do something about it. Have you told Joe?'

Tears threatened then. 'Of course I have.'

'And what was his reaction?'

'Oh, you know Joe, easy going to a fault. He just laughed it off, hugged me and told me not to be so silly.'

Betty nodded. 'I know. Even Harry complains Joe doesn't take anything seriously. But this is serious for you. I'm worried about you, girl. Did you say you wanted to get married?'

I remembered that conversation only too well. 'Of course. A simple Registry Office wedding, I said, and no one else need know.'

'And what did he say?'

'Well I must admit it shook him a bit. But then he said wasn't thirty years of being together enough commitment and what difference would a piece of paper make. I had no answer to that.'

Betty chipped in, 'And how you feel doesn't matter I suppose.'

'Yes.' I could feel the tears starting again so I gathered up the tea things and dumped them in the sink. 'Yes.' I said again. 'That's about the size of it.'

Betty hugged me then and the tears flowed in earnest.

'My dear Sheila, then we'll just have to come up with something that will change his mind.'

❧

A few days later, over lunch, Betty revealed her master plan as she called it. Joe was due to retire the following year and the firm were planning a leaving do at the end of February around the time of my sixtieth birthday. Two milestones; no wonder I was tearful. As it was a leap year, she'd decided it would be the perfect opportunity for me to do the proposing. But, she reasoned, it had to be in a situation he couldn't wriggle out of just by saying 'no' or laughing the whole thing off. So she'd come up with Joe's leaving do as the perfect time. Harry, she said was all for it and would prime the party organisers. All they needed was for me to agree to pop the question in public.

It sounded simple didn't it, fool-proof even. But as it happened it didn't go quite as Betty had planned.

❧

As the days of January slipped by, to say I was getting nervous was putting it mildly. If it hadn't been for Betty reassuring and promising nothing could go wrong, I wouldn't have gone through with it. Panic really set in under the hair-dryer on the morning of the party.

'It's no use Betty,' I wailed. 'What if he says 'no' in front of all those people, it will be so humiliating.'

Betty grinned. 'Trust me, he's not going to say no.'

I wasn't convinced. I couldn't remember the last time I'd felt so nervous. I felt sick and my fingers just wouldn't cooperate as I struggled into my clothes. But I must admit in my new dress, hair and make-up immaculate, I felt good. I must have looked good too because Joe whistled as I went downstairs.

'Who are you?' he said. 'And what have you done to my Sheila?'

That made me giggle. 'Don`t be daft Joe.'

I looked at him all dressed up in his best suit, smiling and seeming to be completely at ease. 'How do you feel Joe?'

'What do you mean? I feel great.'

'About tonight I mean. It`s the end of something for you. How does that feel?'

He thought for a moment. 'Like it's not the end but more the start of something new and exciting.' I felt a jerk of unease and hoped the evenings events weren't going to shatter his mood.

≈

I was surprised when the taxi pulled up outside a hotel on the outskirts of town.

'What are we doing here Joe? Don`t you usually have leaving do's at the factory?'

'Not this evening. The canteen's being decorated so we're having it here. Posh or what?'

'Oh, definitely posh.'

I'm not sure what I was expecting, a conference room perhaps, certainly something large enough to accommodate all the people I thought would be there. Instead we were shown into a small, select dining room, the table laid for what was surely far too few guests. I looked frantically at Betty who just shrugged her shoulders. I thought she was as puzzled as I was. Everybody was grinning, including Joe. I was handed a glass of champagne. I took one small sip. Bewildered and shaking, I couldn`t think what was going on. Then Joe took my hand and led me to a small table at the back of the room and everybody started clapping. I remember looking at Joe to ask him what was happening when he went down on one knee. I think my mouth fell open at that point. This wasn't supposed to happen. It should have been me down on one knee.

Joe clasped both my hands in his. 'Sheila, love of my life, will you do me the honour of becoming my wife?'

I don't remember how long I stood there trying to take it all in. Long enough for the tears to start. I couldn't speak. I couldn't breathe. Joe tugging on my hands brought me to earth and I think I must have said 'yes' because a huge cheer went up and Joe was hugging me and I was laughing and crying at the same time.

But it didn't end there. Between them, Harry and Joe had arranged for the Registrar to be present and we were married with Harry and Betty as witnesses. The hotel had provided the wedding breakfast, only it was really supper and instead of a leaving present everyone had contributed to a honeymoon in Paris.

I spent the rest of the evening in a daze and it wasn't until we'd returned from honeymoon that Betty told me the whole story. She had omitted to tell me the second part of her grand plan. Harry had been persuaded to 'spill the beans' to Joe who had at first been furious.

'What's the big deal?' he'd wanted to know. 'I'm not going to run away now, we've been together too long, got too much history for that.' Harry had been very patient and had pointed out that if Joe really loved me, was it too much to ask, if it was what I wanted. He'd also said that we had a lot of years ahead of us and if it made for a happy old age, what was stopping him.

I still don't know what finally persuaded Joe, he's not saying! But I understand now what he meant by his retirement being the start of something new and exciting. I hope it will be a long and beautiful adventure.

Anne Abbinnett

Memories

A castle stands guard
on a lonely hill,
the richness of the Cheshire plain
spread out beneath its crumbling shell.
A green and vibrant land
edged with the poking spires
of urban living,
the greedy towers of industry
leeching off leafy byways.

A cold wind blows
strongly from the east,
and my thoughts
tumble and fall
down through the years.

Another castle under
a lowering northern sky
standing sentinel
against the force of time.
We wandered through the gloomy halls
hands entwined,
from battered walls
surveyed village and farm
nestled in the fold of hills.
Easy promises made
there was nothing left to say.

Shoulders hunched against the wind
our fingers touched
in a last goodbye.

A stiff breeze brings rain,
or are they bitter tears
of memory
that dampen my cheeks.

Doug Barratt

Cyril's Journey

Cyril sat, as usual, in the last carriage of the Bakerloo Line train. He always travelled in the last carriage - it was nearest to the exit at his final destination, Harrow and Wealdstone, at the end of the line. He always made the same journey - Central Line from St Paul's and change at Oxford Circus.

He was a creature of habit. Now forty-eight years old and still a bachelor, he had devoted his life to his profession. With a good maths degree under his belt he had taken a job as an accountant in the City at the age of twenty-three and worked his way up the accountancy ladder to become chief accountant at the firm of solicitors on Ludgate Hill where he had worked for the past fifteen years.

Cyril looked up from the Evening Standard's *Suduko* puzzle he had been studying, surveyed the carriage and his fellow passengers and glanced at his watch. 9.50pm - he would normally be home by now watching some documentary on the Discovery Channel, having already made himself a sandwich an hour or so earlier in the evening. These days he usually had a good, long, lunch out with one or two of his colleagues so did not usually have much of an appetite when he arrived home.

But this week was different. It was the end of March and next week the new tax year would begin. Every accountant in the country was busy number crunching, so for this week, and probably most of next week as well, Cyril would be working a few hours overtime - unpaid, of course.

Travelling at this time of the evening had its advantages. Usually he was lucky if he got a seat before the train was well past Baker

Street but tonight he found one easily. There was the normal coming and going of passengers until the train reached Paddington from which point his fellow travellers mainly consisted of early evening drinkers who had now abandoned their West End haunts, or late night shoppers who had spent the last couple of hours with their friends in *Starbucks*.

Cyril had become oblivious to the train's usual stops at Warwick Avenue, Maida Vale and Kilburn Park, a few passengers being disgorged at each stop. He gradually became aware, however, of the group of young men at the far end of the carriage. It was the sound of empty beer cans being kicked about that he noticed first but then the raised voices of the group became apparent. Cyril put it down to normal, boisterous behaviour of twenty-somethings. He noticed that other passengers seemed to be reseating themselves away from the group.

Queen's Park, Kensal Green stations - most of the passengers had now left the train or moved to the next carriage. Cyril tried to focus his attention on the financial pages he was now reading in the paper whilst still trying to keep a wary eye on the group of lads. He had now read the last paragraph four times but nothing was registering. He did not like the thoughts entering his head of the situation that may possibly arise. He sank into his seat as though trying to make himself invisible. Should he leave the train at the next station? How far *was* the next station? The train slowed as it pulled into Willesden Junction.

Cyril breathed a sigh of relief as the group made to leave the train but the 'high fives' and a loud exclamation of, 'Catch you later, Bro', alerted him to the fact that he was now alone in the carriage with the two lads who had stayed on the train. The next stop was Harlesden. With its high ethnic population this is where Cyril was expecting the pair to disembark but the train was moving inexorably slowly. An adverse signal caused it to grind to a halt.

The lads, who had been in deep conversation since their friends had left the train, moved purposefully down the carriage towards Cyril whose mouth suddenly became very dry and he tried to sink even deeper into his seat.

With a jolt the train resumed its journey and pulled slowly into Harlesden station. Cyril decided that now was a good time to get off the train and as the doors swished open he stuffed his newspaper into his briefcase and rose from his seat but his way to the door was blocked by the six foot muscular frame of the taller of the two lads whilst the other one left the train.

Cyril sank dejectedly back into his seat.

'Hey, Lionel, go for it, man,' he heard the departee shout as the doors closed trapping Cyril in his metal prison.

'Then there were two,' he thought to himself. And 'go for' what? Robbery, murder - his own murder? Stay calm, he tried to tell himself. What deed had the two lads cooked up? Cyril felt sure that, whatever it was, it involved himself - and he was the intended victim. But maybe he was blowing things up out of all proportion. He decided that sitting quietly looking as nonchalant as possible may be the answer. He retrieved his newspaper from his briefcase. Further thoughts were interrupted.

'Oi, you. Gimme a light,' ordered the deep, dark voice of the menacing figure who had now slumped into the seat directly opposite Cyril.

'S-s-sorry, I don't smoke,' stammered Cyril in a barely audible mumble. Something told Cyril that this was not the right time to remind Lionel that smoking was not allowed on the tube.

Lionel sat, long legs outstretched and his dark eyes glaring, boring into Cyril's puny body. Cyril fumbled with his newspaper. Time dragged. Could this train go any slower? Slowly - very slowly - Stonebridge Park, Wembley Central and North Wembley stations were mentally ticked off the list in Cyril's head, but with them came no fellow travellers. He pondered - where were reinforcements when you needed them? Cyril wondered to himself why he hadn't made a bolt for the door at one of these stops but he felt sure that Lionel's athletic body would be behind him and overcome him within seconds. No - better to play it cool for now. Lionel must be getting off the train very soon. After all, there were only three stops left. Three stops to familiarity and safety.

Cyril tried to shut further dark thoughts from his mind but was brought back to reality by a loud click from Lionel's direction. The bright carriage lights glinted on the five inch blade of the flick knife which Lionel now brandished in his huge hand. Cyril sat transfixed, thoughts racing through his head. He could see the headlines on tomorrow's edition of the very paper he was reading - 'City accountant in tube stabbing,' or 'Murder on the Bakerloo Line.'

He hoped that Lionel could not see the sweat forming on his balding head, know how his pulse was racing and his hands shaking or sense the sick feeling in the pit of his stomach. Wasn't adrenalin supposed to pump through one's body? Fight or flight? – wasn't that the saying? Locked in this steel box, flight was not possible and, as for fight, this was something he had never done and would not know where to start. His pathetic, skinny, five foot six inches of scrawny body which required a pair of glasses to even see anything was definitely not a fighting machine.

Lionel couldn't see Cyril sweating but he knew very well that he would be. Look at that pathetic wretch, thought Lionel. Big shot banker going home to his big house, little wife and average 2.4 spoiled brats. I'll bet they don't have to sleep top-to-tail with three others in the same bed like I used to have to. I'm going to teach this idiot a lesson - just scare him, shake him up a bit - maybe come away with a Rolex or a credit card or two - maybe even his car if he's feeling really generous towards his less well-off travelling companion. I can take him dead easy - like putty in my hands. What can he do? He's a loser – and I'm not afraid of anything.

Cyril considered pulling the emergency handle - but what then? Lionel would simply put the knife away and sit grinning and ask the railway staff what all the fuss was about. He had not actually made any physical threats.

South Kenton station came and went. Only two more stops. Still Lionel sat opposite, eyeballing Cyril and now casually cleaning his finger nails with the sharp point of his knife. Cyril sat with his briefcase crushed under his arm, subconsciously trying to give Lionel the impression that it was actually worth something. If the necessity arose, perhaps he could barter for his life with it - together with his wallet, credit cards and antiquated mobile phone. His newspaper lay discarded on the seat beside him.

'Ah, - Kenton station. Surely Lionel must get off here,' thought Cyril, his hopes rising, only to be dashed again as the doors closed whilst Lionel still sat opposite, now with a crazed look in his eyes and with a twisted grin on his mean-looking lips.

Cyril's thoughts turned to his 'escape' from the station at Harrow. He felt sure that Lionel would follow him up the stairs and out of the station before he pounced. He must find a way to alert somebody to his dire situation. There was the ticket inspector who was always on duty at the ticket barrier or the clerk in the ticket office. He would stop for a prolonged conversation with one of these whilst Lionel would, hopefully, be gone on his way.

The train slowed and came to a gentle halt. Cyril rose and made his way to the door making certain that he did not step on Lionel's giant feet. As he passed he heard Lionel mutter, 'Watch your back, wimp.'

Cyril hurried up the stairs but could hear Lionel's heavy footsteps close behind him. The ticket inspector's box was now closed as was its adjoining gate. Cyril's hands were shaking uncontrollably as he fumbled with his ticket trying to get it into the slot in the automatic ticket barrier. The gate swung open and Cyril glanced at the ticket office window. His heart sank as he read the word, 'Closed' on the blind inside the window.

He rushed towards the exit and could no longer hear Lionel's footsteps. He probably did not have a ticket and could not get through the barrier. Cyril glanced behind him in time to see Lionel vault over the ticket barrier and resume his relentless pursuit.

Cyril was now in a state of panic. To reach the bus stop he had to cross the poorly lit car park – an ideal place for a bloody murder. As he went through the station doorway he remembered the old-fashioned telephone box twenty yards to the right - his final refuge - or his final resting place. As he dashed for the phone box he could hear Lionel running, rapidly closing the distance between them. Cyril yanked open the door of the phone box and lifted the phone.

No time to find coins, he thought. I'll have to call 999 - no coins needed for that. As Cyril's finger hit the first button, the door swung open and there stood Lionel, filling the doorway, his knife held menacingly, pointing in the direction of Cyril's navel. The newspaper headline flashed through Cyril's head again - 'City accountant in phone box murder.' Cyril cowered, trembling in the corner of the box as he grovelled.

'What do you want?' he croaked. 'Here, take my case. You can have my wallet and mobile as well - just leave me alone - please.'

Lionel rolled his eyes upwards as if to say 'Do you think that's what I really want?' but as he did so he let out an almighty scream, his huge, golf ball eyes almost popped out of his face and he started to shake uncontrollably. His knife clattered to the floor as he stood transfixed like a statue. Cyril's gaze followed Lionel's until he saw, dangling six inches above Lionel's upturned face, his saviour - a spider no more than two inches long.

In an instant Cyril reached up and scooped up the spider, although he would admit that he didn't much care for them himself, and, as he did so, Lionel turned on his heels and started to run screaming back towards the station entrance. Cyril ran after him triumphantly waving his new found friend above his head. Lionel was nowhere to be seen.

Doug Barratt

A Magic Night

Very little crime went on in the little township of Rockway, perched on a small headland at the end of a two mile causeway which nosed its way into the Gulf of Mexico from the Louisiana mainland.

What crime there was, which was spasmodic and never too serious, usually turned out to be the work of the Brewhouse Gang - a couple of dozen bored teenagers who were hardly the world's brightest criminals and who were usually rounded up within a couple of days, slapped on the wrist and allowed to carry on regardless.

The town's grapevine had recently been busy carrying news of regular seaborne deliveries of wooden crates arriving at the customs office which sat alongside the town's small fishing harbour. Occasionally such movement would be triggered by a successful contraband raid by the local US Coastguard patrol boat. The rumours had now reached the Brewhouse Gang - they decided it would definitely be worth taking a closer look.

The time was set - 2 am on a November, Saturday morning. A storm was preparing to unleash itself on the little town. The wind had whipped up into a frenzy sending waves crashing against the harbour wall and salty spray into the air towards the customs house. The gang, now huddling against the side of the building seeking what limited shelter it offered, were gathered, prepared for action. Inadequately armed with nothing more than crowbars, torches, a few pairs of pliers and a collection of shoulder bags in which to stash the cigarettes, liquor or drugs they hoped to find, they edged their way in the darkness towards the building's flimsy rear door. Getting into the building was no great challenge - the inadequacies of the antiquated security system were well known - and this by far from being their first visit.

At 2.10 they were all assembled in the musty, old, brick building surveying by torchlight a large stack of wooden crates of varying shapes and sizes piled into a corner of the warehouse. These were not the usual uniform shape of cigarette containers or bottle cases. No, these had a strange, sinister look about them.

Undaunted, Richie, the self-appointed leader of the gang was the first to make a move. He pulled aside a small crate from the foot of the pile and levered it open with his crowbar. The contents were small bundles neatly wrapped in brown paper. Could it be banknotes? As he stripped away the paper he held aloft his prize – a strange pack of playing cards. He stared unblinkingly at the top card and read the word, 'Death'. A loud peal of thunder from the tempest, now building to its climax, reverberated through the building. In a rage Richie threw the cards into the air, ripping into the next bundle to find the same contents which triggered the same response. He threw the remains of the crate to one side which seemed to be a signal for the rest of the gang to get stuck into the pile.

A few more small crates were ripped apart - packs of standard playing cards as well as more of the Tarot cards which Richie had discovered. All were discarded with distain. The gang moved on to some of the larger crates but with no more satisfaction. Moments later the floor was a sea of costumes - wizards' outfits, conjurors' costumes, African witch doctor's attire and some very skimpy ladies' costumes which did actually spark some momentary interest in some of the gang members, but were, nevertheless, discarded.

As the gang pulled frantically at the foot of the pile a large crate dislodged itself from the top of the heap and crashed down the wooden hillside and onto one of the gang members. As it hit him the weight of it killed him outright. The crate split open on the floor next to him and spilled its contents of heavy chains and padlocks. The storm outside continued unabated, the wind's tentacles ripping at the corrugated iron roof of the building as though it was desperate to somehow reach the gang.

A few members of the gang attempted to revive their friend but, realising it was a lost cause, abandoned him and returned to their assault on the wooden pyramid.

Very gingerly they lifted another large crate down from the pile. They prised open the side of the crate about a foot - just enough room for a human skull to make its escape and roll across the floor. One of the gang let out a terrified scream, which was lost in the crescendo of the howling gale, and bolted for the opposite corner of the room where he sat shaking like a leaf. The escaped skull was followed by a large selection of bones and several more skulls as the side of the crate fell away.

Richie was, by now, wondering what on earth they had discovered. Whatever it was it created a feeling of foreboding amongst his gang who were now lacking their usual bravado.

Next crate - a small one containing dolls. Could be children's toys - but not these. Who would give a child one of these with long, vicious looking pins stuck right through them?

The gang now uncovered another large crate which was emitting a very strange subdued shuffling noise. With some trepidation and one gang member on each side of the crate, they levered up the lid. As they lifted the lid together they were overwhelmed by a cloud of white feathers and dust as a flock of two hundred white doves made good their escape from the crate and swooped around the warehouse diving frighteningly close to the heads of the gang members who fell to their knees and covered their heads.

Richie had seen enough - almost. 'Two more crates and we're out of here, lads,' he announced.

The penultimate crate - more livestock. This time about a hundred and fifty, fluffy white rabbits which hopped around dementedly, getting under the feet of the gang members.

With a final flourish Richie brought down his crowbar on the crate on which he had chosen to end his spree. This one was about four feet long, a foot deep and a foot wide. As it split open the light from the torches reflected brightly from a set of shining steel sword blades.

'At last - something to make the evening worthwhile,' he exclaimed as he tossed each gang member a sword. There were just enough for the spoils to be evenly shared.

'Just in case we need to fight our way out of here,' he joked. 'Let's go,' he urged, giving a cursory glance to Mac who wasn't going anywhere, dead and buried as he was, beneath the pile of chains.

The sight which greeted Ted Bronovsky, the town's customs officer, when he opened the customs shed the following morning made him heave. One look at the carnage inside the shed and he slammed and locked the door, made his way back to his office and picked up the phone to call Sheriff Jay Richardson over on the mainland.

Jay answered the phone and could hear Bronovsky's voice trembling.

'Hi Ted, you got a problem over there?'

'Yeah, Jay. Just a slight one. You'd better get over here real quick.'

'Ok Ted, just give me a clue.'

'Well, it's to do with the stuff I've had holed up in the warehouse for the last couple of days. You know - the stuff for the Magic Convention up at the Gulf Hotel next weekend. Seems like someone broke in last night - our usual Brewhouse friends. I know it's them - or, rather, *was* them. They're all lying on the floor, each one with a sword neatly shoved down his gullet. There's a guy dead under a pile of chains, bones and skulls all over the floor, together with some real weird clothes. And the place is like a bloody zoo - literally. White doves and rabbits all over the place, all splattered with blood. I guarantee you've never seen anything like it.'

Richardson's car screeched to a halt outside Ted's office barely five minutes after he had replaced the receiver.

Ted Bronovsky unlocked the warehouse door and swung it open, reluctant to look again at the sight which had caused him to throw up earlier. Richardson took a look inside the building and then turned to look incredulously at his friend.

'Ted, what the hell were you on last night? There's nothing here.'

And he was right. There was nothing there at all. The inside of the warehouse was completely empty and clean as a new pin.

Lynne Stokoe
A Walk Across the Bay

Early morning, the sky is wide
Heading across to Kents Bank
From scenic Arnside

Laughing, smiling, chatting crowd
Clothed in colours bright
Heads against the wind, bowed

Through the day they walk
Mud bespattered all;
Soon too tired to talk

The line stretches out across the sand
All around, the shifting water flows
In the distance, solid land

Morecambe Bay - a wide and vast expanse
Teeming with life unseen
Washing in and out to the sea's dance

The walkers follow the certain guide
Young, old and in-between
Safe from the racing, wicked tide

The sun sets, the line wends
It straggles homeward, weary
The walk is done, the day ends

Lynne Stokoe

Happy Heart

I left my heart in Bradford Royal Infirmary in 2008. It's now beating away steadily in one James Alexander Ramsey who lives in Inverkip on the Clyde - which is ironical because I'd been there just twelve months before.

❦

Whilst on a business trip in the south of Spain, late in 2006, I'd met a Scot called Andrew Rennie who lived in Port Glasgow, very near to Inverkip. We got chatting in a restaurant as he too was dining on his own and was only there to close down his holiday house for the winter. It turned out that he had a son who had been suffering with severe headaches for two years, and Glasgow Royal Infirmary had drawn a blank as to the cause. Andrew was taking him south the following week, to the specialist neurology department at Fazakerley, a suburb of Liverpool.

He asked if I knew Merseyside and I told him that Liverpool is my home town and I knew exactly where the hospital is situated. I even recommended a hotel that he could stay in for the week. When I got up to leave we exchanged phone numbers and made arrangements to meet, and I ended up giving him a tour of the city.

❦

The hospital didn't find any answers for his son though. From my new position in life (or more accurately, in death) I can see exactly what's the matter with Kenny but it'll be a while before the medics finally see the light. I'm pleased to think that very soon Kenny will be rid of those crippling headaches and will be back working again. This fourth dimension has some good points, you know.

※

Anyway, Andrew and I kept in touch and I went to visit him in Port Glasgow. He wanted to return my kindness, he said, though I don't remember doing much apart from the city tour and a few drinks. I always loved Scotland and the sea and had envied Andrew his house, high on the hill, on that day in May 2007. He and his wife showed me the local sights and we ended up eating a very good steak in Inverkip - which is why I had been there. The long arm of coincidence.
    Little did I know that I would never see them, Port Glasgow or Inverkip again. Not in that life.

※

In May 2007, I went to Bradford for a conference, walked out of the hotel, talking on my mobile as usual. I didn't hear the truck career out of control, otherwise I might have jumped clear. It hit me and knocked me sideways and I landed in a heap, my skull crushed.

※

They found the donor card of course. Several people had life-changing operations in the next twenty-four hours using various bits of me, but I left my heart in James Alexander Ramsey, who has a spectacular view of the Clyde from his front windows in Inverkip. My heart is happy.

Lynne Stokoe
Hope

The museum was at the other side of the city and he could only spare an hour before taking a taxi to the airport. The day had been eaten up with all the usual meetings, a total waste of time in his opinion. They'd even started having meetings about meetings. Were there too many? Not enough? Should more or less people be invited? Yadda, yadda, yadda.

Joe's mind kept wandering all day long, he just wanted to get to the museum to see the painting, the painting he'd loved all his life but never thought he would ever see. The print had hung in his grandfather, Tom's shed until the day he died and Joe had inherited the print - well more accurately, he had said he would like to have it. The rest of the family just shrugged, none of them wanted it. Tom didn't have much to leave, he had given most of his things away over the years and lived very simply. His most precious possessions were his garden tools - he spent long hours on his allotment even in the winter and had made numerous friends there. They had all come to the funeral bringing huge bunches of flowers - and baskets of vegetables which had gone to the food bank at the back of the church. Joe sighed. Who would have thought that food banks would be in every city, town and village in Great Britain in the 21st century? Not his grandad anyway.

Tom had somehow managed to survive the Second World War and to live until the grand age of ninety-three, but his own father Alfred had died in the trenches only four months after his call up. So he had never met his son, who had been born a few weeks later. Tom often said that very few lessons had been learned from that war or the one that followed. He didn't talk about his own war experiences, but he had the print which he said gave him hope for the future. It was Monet's *Poppy Field* and wasn't even in colour, but was actually a black and white photograph of the painting. Peter, one of his old school friends, had lived in Paris for a few years because his grandmother was French. He had brought a few of the prints home and given them to his friends - nobody really knew how he had got them.

    Joe's grandad told him about the poppies growing in the fields of Flanders, and although the painting was done long before the wars and was actually painted in France, it still, for him, symbolised hope after the wars. That reclaiming of the land, that making life colourful again after the long, dark days of war, always remembered in monotone. Even when the skies were blue there was a grey feel to the air, the green of the grass muted by the dust of battle. Joe had grown up with these stories, sitting in the little shed with his granddad.

⁂

Joe wanted to see the painting, he wanted to see it in colour - and here he was, in Paris for a few weeks with Mac, his boss - and this was his last day. He had to seize the opportunity, he may never come back to Paris again. He glanced at his watch for the umpteenth time. Would the day never end? It had been like this all week - and then there had been meals with clients until it was too late to go to the museum. This evening there was a late night opening and here was his chance at last.

    He had said goodbye to his boss at 4pm because Mac was catching a plane to Edinburgh, leaving Joe to 'tie up the loose ends' as he put it. It was now 6pm and his own flight was due to leave at 8.30, so he was on a tight schedule.

⁂

He got to the Musee D'Orsay quicker than he had expected, as the Metro was so fast. He was walking through the door at twenty-past six. He looked at the museum guide, found out where the painting was hung and taking a deep breath he headed for the fifth floor. He entered the room and looked wildly around amongst the Impressionist paintings in the first room. Not here. He almost ran into the second room, his mind whirling - what if it wasn't there? What if they were giving it a rest or whatever they do? He knew nothing about museums and art galleries really, but he did know there were stacks of paintings in the National Gallery that hadn't been on show for years.

Then finally, in the third room he came to, he saw it. Not as big as he had expected, not even as brightly coloured, but oh how it spoke to him. It was such a peaceful picture, the woman with her child strolling through the field full of flowers, that blue sky with high clouds. It had an atmosphere about it, it made him want to be in such a place.

Tom had loved growing flowers as well as vegetables. It was a rare week when he had no colour on his allotment. It started with the snowdrops in late January and continued until the hellebores and witch hazels of December. Now, Joe understood why the print being black and white was of no consequence to his Grandad. The hope in the picture was symbolic. The real thing happened every year on his council allotment. Every spring was hope - a new beginning. Proof that wars would come and wars would go - but where there is any green shoot, any winter flower, any autumn crocus and indeed any summer poppy, then there is hope for humankind.

He stood for some time looking at the picture and then it was time to leave. His quest was ended. He had a plane to catch.

Lynne Stokoe
Oswald's Story

It had all started with Mr Rabitovich, Oswald's agent. The first job he'd had was as an extra in *'Watership Down'* - the stage production. Mr R had needed to find sixty rabbits of varying sizes and shapes and discipline was required. Well, being disciplined was second nature to rabbits - an absolute essential for survival. Only a few silly ones ignored the rules and they paid the price. So Mr R didn't struggle to find his extras and he had his eye on Oswald from the outset.

The rabbit was big and handsome and his pale, grey fur was always silky and shining. He was soon in great demand for the many roles he was auditioned to play and was amazed at the amount of work there was out there. He'd been in panto of course, *'Alice in Wonderland.'* He'd been given the watch as a souvenir, although it hadn't been much use in the burrow where they were on Bobtail Time.

Easter had been very busy too. He had been the pack leader for twenty small, brown bunnies, specially chosen for their cuddly looks. He'd come to loathe the smell of chocolate though, never mind the taste.

Still, the kids had loved the freebies. After that he'd auditioned for a job that involved being chased by dogs. It had sounded like hard work to Oswald and he hadn't been interested really. In the end, the job had gone to a large, imposing rabbit called Harold whom Oswald privately thought looked more like a hare. He had never seen Harold at the auditions since then, which was a tad worrying.

Some jobs were just plain embarrassing. Once he had had to get dressed up as *Bunnikins* and he'd felt daft in a frock. He'd enjoyed being a body double for *Bugs Bunny* though - and doing some footwork for *Thumper* to give him a rest. Bonus carrots for both jobs had kept the entire burrow happy for days.

A few weeks before that, there had been a TV advert with Jamie Oliver. He'd always thought Jamie was a gentle kind of guy. Rabbit Pie indeed! Hetty had been upset for days afterwards and the new litter wouldn't stop crying. He had shuddered for a long time at the memory.

On the whole, he preferred a personal performance job where he was the only rabbit required. He'd absolutely loved the job with Magic McIver. He'd always thought that the old trick of the magician producing the rabbit out of the hat was a bit naff, but McIver was brilliant and the audience never tired of seeing Oswald jumping out of the hat in his scarlet cloak and bowing gracefully to them all. It was very sad that Magic had taken a job on a cruise ship and Oswald's injections had not been up to date. Anyway it was just as well - an ocean between him and his beloved family was just not on.

꙳

In October the nights had been getting much colder. Oswald wished sometimes that he'd never gone into this game. He could have been quite happy beside the cabbage fields for all his life, with Hetty and the many children they'd had together, although he was hard pushed to remember all their names. (He had spent so many days away from the burrow).

His stress levels had gone through the roof when Mr Rabitovich had announced that he wanted a larger percentage of Oswald's earnings. In justification, he had also announced that he'd been approached by a TV company in London who wanted Oswald for the lead roles in two productions. First of all there was to be '*Roger Rabbit - the Musical*'. 'It was a wonderful opportunity' he'd said. There'd be a spin off - an entire album of rabbit themed hits.
Imagine! Well, Oswald couldn't imagine. Apart from '*Run Rabbit Run*' and that awful Chas and Dave song he couldn't think of any more songs about rabbits. He couldn't sing either, which apparently hadn't occurred to any of them.

Then - Oswald had been staggered at the idea – a pilot for a series called ' *Barer Rabbit goes Forth*'. For goodness sake, who'd ever heard of *Brer Rabbit*? He'd gone out of fashion fifty years ago at least. Oswald had only ever read about him in '*The Ancient Chronicles of Rabbitdom.*' He really had not wanted to leave the comfortable and luxurious burrow, or to disrupt his family. They were all living very well, they didn't need any more. He hadn't wanted to go down to London for twice the rewards although he didn't mind about Mr R getting a bigger cut. He had thought hard about it all. Was he ready to give it all up?. Go back to scratching a living in the fields, cabbages, lettuce, carrots for a treat. Always dodging the farmer's gun, the traps. The odd cat that was almost as fast as him.

Maybe he could do without an agent – he had dismissed this idea as soon as it entered his mind, he knew that without Mr R he would get no work. He knew he had to be strong and say what he wanted and not to be bullied into going to London.

༺

The next day he had met Mr R in the The Meadows. His agent had been still buzzing with adrenalin and hadn't been able to hide his glee at the thought of the wonderful deal he'd found for Oswald. He hadn't noticed Oswald's lack of enthusiasm as he expounded the details of the contract, the lucrative terms, the influential people involved etc. Oswald had just sat there, saying nothing. The agent had finally run out of steam and then had looked at Oswald enquiringly.

'What's up?' he had said 'Deal not good enough?'

Oswald had sighed. 'I'm sorry boss', he said. 'You'll have to get another rabbit, one who can sing for a start. I've had a good run and I'm grateful to you for everything, but I'm very happy doing the routine stuff, really I am. There's plenty of up and coming youngsters out there who'd be delighted to go to London. Not me though. I had my turn in the spotlight when I was with Magic, it was good, but I don't miss it'

Rabitovich had seen his dream of fame and riches fading fast. He'd been furious and had started on at Oswald about his ingratitude, how was he going to find another rabbit with his looks, what was he going to say to the guys in London and so on. Oswald had looked at him, hard.

'Are you serious,' he said? 'Do you know how many rabbits there are out there?'

Mr R was cross. 'Of course I know,' he said, 'Do you think I'm stupid? Point is, they're not you, star quality is rare, ask Simon Cowell. If you won't do it, I don't know what I'll do. I can't force you,' he finished miserably. He stared into his pint, the very picture of despair.

'Well,' Oswald had told him, 'I guess I owe you. 'I'll take the job as long as you get another rabbit to do the songs, tell the guy I'll have to mime. And I want to bring the wife and kids for the duration; I'm not leaving them behind. So make sure there's plenty of room please, there'll be another litter along shortly. Get the contracts drawn up, we're in business.'

‽

That was last year. Oswald's last contract. . Mr R got what he wanted, the fame, the wealth, the lifestyle. He's in LA now. Oswald's back up north in the old burrow. He has made enough from the shows to keep him and the family in comfort for the rest of their days. He had had a great understudy, a big guy called Hank who was an instant hit when Oswald's contracts came to an end.

Boy could he sing! He was great as *Brer Rabbit* too, a natural comic. Oswald felt that he too had made a good comic, he got the timing right. Like his retirement from showbiz.

That's the end of my story. Sorry to have rabbited on.

Lynne Stokoe
Space

'Space, I need space,' she said
But I knew what was inside her head

'I'm tired of talking,' she said
But *I* knew our marriage was dead

Space is a euphemism for goodbye
It's a breath on the wind and a sigh
And when did we start to use space
For getting us out of a place?
Is space so elusive and rare
That we use it to undo a pair?

'Space? You can have it,' I say
'I never did take it away
I'm sick of the talking as well
And I'm hearing the toll of the bell'

Chase the space and win the race
Trace the case for changing base

S   p   a   c   e   d

Out

Lynne Stokoe
The Village at the End of the World

Marietta stood looking out of the window at the top of the tower. She watched the people streaming up the narrow road toward the mountain, the mysterious mountain which had fascinated people for generations. She had been watching for three hours, only stopping to make a quick herb omelette for lunch and then she was back at her post. It had started with a trickle and now it was a heaving surge of humanity. They had been coming all morning and each time she thought it was dying away, when she looked again, the road was as crowded as ever.

There was only one week to go before the end of the world. Her family lived in Alet les Bains, not far away. She had married an Englishman who had come to this part of south west France to paint ...his parents had died when he was in his twenties, leaving him financially secure but totally bereft. It had been so sudden. First his father had suffered a massive heart attack and died on his way home from work. His mother, always fragile, had taken her own life six weeks later, being incapable of facing life without her beloved husband. Francis was an only child, as both of his parents had been. .....With no grandparents, aunts, uncles or cousins, Francis had felt alone in the world but at least he had the money to start this new life in France. He was happy in the small village in the foothills of the Pyrenees, where the light was perfect on so many days of the year. .....He and Marietta had not had any children, but had three small dogs who scampered up and down their unusual dwelling. The Tower had been empty for years but was sturdily built. The owner was a local landowner whose main income was from his wineries in Limoux which produced the sparkling wine which is so famous. (Although

not everybody realises that this was the first place in France to produce such a wine - the Champagne region caught up much later.) Marietta's family links persuaded M. Gilbert to sell them the tower. They had made it into a comfortable home and it suited them.
.....Marietta picked up her sewing but was totally unable to concentrate. All she could think of was the events that were unfolding here in the village, her home for so many years. She had never really believed the prophesy, she thought it was all a silly story. The priest said it was just superstitious nonsense but then there were a lot of folk who thought that about the church's teachings. France was fast becoming a secular country in every way and not just because of the constitution. *Liberté, fraternité, equalité*. Marietta sometimes wondered what kind of country France would be if the revolution hadn't happened.

She gazed out again. Still the people came, filing past the tower, their cars left behind in the fields lower down the slopes - those who had come by car that is. Others had just got a flight to Montpellier and had hired somebody to drive them to the village. Some had come on the fast train from Paris. All of them believed implicitly in the prophesy, this was to be the only village left when the world came to an end. They were coming in their droves to be saved.

Marietta touched the two growths that had started on her back in recent weeks. They were getting bigger every day. She hadn't mentioned this to Francis until it became impossible to hide. They had looked at each other with growing awareness and disbelief. Marietta was growing wings! She had always known, since she was a small child, that she was a descendant. The family were very proud of this fact. She just thought, 'So what?' It was all such a long time ago.
.....Marietta was born in Rennes le Chateau and was a descendant of Mary Magdalene and Jesus her husband. There were not many left of course after the Crusades and the Inquisition but some had got away and had gone into hiding. They had moved away and then gradually drifted back when the heat was off. The Cathars had been ruthlessly hunted and almost completely extinguished, but still the legends remained, even now in the 21st Century.

The prophesy was something everyone for miles around knew about. It said that the end of the world would be next week and only the village she lived in now would be left, when everything else had been destroyed. It also said that the leader would be a descendant and would have the gift of flight. Ridiculous. She and her friends had agreed. Now this.

Obviously the prophesy was true, she was the one destined to lead the people to the mountain top and there they would dwell until the world as they knew it was gone. Her wings were a sign for everyone who came here to see that she was the one. She was horrified. She didn't want this thing that was happening. She just wanted her peaceful life with Francis, her sewing that earned her a small living, his painting, their life in the tower surrounded by the green, sloping meadows of summertime. In the winter the gentle snows and the autumn fades of yellowing leaves. And oh, the spring. The march of March, rampaging in with the cold wind and then by the month's end the gentle breeze, the new warmth and then April's flower filled fields and May's emerald shading. If this really was the only village to be saved, she could understand totally why that would be. It was so beautiful.

~

Only one week before everything changed. Her wings were fully grown. She had retreated to the top floor of the tower as they grew and grew. Francis had been doing all the errands that she normally did, he told the neighbours in the village - when they asked - that Marietta was very busy making a bridal gown and six bridesmaids dresses for a young woman in Montelieu, who had been let down by the dressmaker she had hired originally. It was a good enough story. Soon enough they would all know the truth.

~

She looked out of the window again. She heaved an enormous sigh. The wings were heavy but she needed to do it. She climbed onto the stone sill. She took a deep breath and then, she leapt out of the window. The wings whispered and then roared and then they were no longer heavy, She was flying and it was glorious, She was soon soaring and swooping over the village, over the rooftops . The crowds of people going up the mountain and those already at the summit could be seen clearly from her vantage point in the cloudless sky.

Now she realised what she must do. She flew over the wintry fields and quietly fluttered to the earth in the cover of some trees. It was growing dark and she crept up to the rear of the tower where Francis was sitting by the fire on the ground floor polishing his shoes, just as he always did. She went inside and put her finger to her lips. He started in surprise and fear when he saw her standing in the kitchen, her wings still red and glowing from the flight.

'Come my love, we must leave here and fly together to the top of the mountain. I have used my wings today and I have seen the future. We are to rule together, for without you I am nothing. Come on, leave all this. We must go now, we have work to do.'

Peter Scarisbrick
Alan's Art

Alan hated homework, and tonight it was as bad as ever - write a list of places where people lived and draw a picture of your favourite one. There would be a star for the boy and the girl with the longest list, and a star for the boy and the girl with the best drawing.

What on earth was the point. Slimy Cyril would win both boys' stars and soppy Selina, his twin, would win the girls'. It happened every week in art; they just couldn't lose. Their dad was an artist who owned the picture and framing shop in the High Street. But most of all, they were very good at drawing.

Alan's Mum's voice yelled up the stairs. 'Have you finished that homework yet? The football starts in five minutes and you're not coming down to watch it until that homework's finished.'

He kicked the bedroom door shut with a bang. He was getting fed up with football anyway. 'Suit yourself,' shouted his mother, 'and stop banging doors.' Alan shook his head in disbelief as downstairs the lounge door slammed shut.

He flopped onto his bed. Next it would be - if you don't finish that homework there is no supper for you tonight - why were Thursday nights so predictable. Then he had a brainwave. He crept onto the landing and listened. '*Eastenders*' was on the telly. He carried on down the stairs, tiptoed past the lounge and into the kitchen - no sweets, no biscuits, not even any cookies. Mum shopped on a Friday: another reason why Thursday nights were rubbish. He looked in the fridge. There wasn't even any yoghurt. The only thing edible in the whole house was a big lump of cheddar cheese. Quickly he sliced off three big chunks and slapped them between two slices of bread. The '*Eastenders*' theme tune drifted out of the lounge.

He'd just stashed his cheese butty under his pillow, when his Mum's head appeared around the bedroom door. She went over to his desk and peered at the blank exercise book and pristine drawing paper.

'No supper for…'

'I know,' yelled Alan.

His mum screwed up her face in her special you-see-if-I-don't-win-this-one frown. 'And, if it's not done by morning,' she said, 'no breakfast either.' She slammed the door behind her. Alan pulled the slightly squashed cheese sandwich from under the pillow and took a big bite. It wasn't much, but there was just a tiny bit of comfort left in life.

When he'd finished he brushed the crumbs off the bed. He lay back with a sigh and stared at the model helicopter suspended from the ceiling over a giant *Lego* oilrig. It was the last thing that his Dad had made with him before he'd left. He opened his bedside drawer and pulled out the secret photograph, the one taken on holiday with his Mum on one side and his Dad on the other.

He went over to his desk, smoothed out the drawing paper and picked up the pencil. He closed his eyes and tried to imagine what he wanted to draw. He was about to give up when a crazy idea came to him. Say the pencil was magic. He held it gently on the paper and emptied his mind. His hand moved. He didn't stop to think; he just concentrated on the picture in his head, and the pencil in his hand dashed around the paper. As suddenly as it had begun, his hand stopped. He opened his fingers and let the pencil fall. He rubbed his eyes. It was like waking from a dream. Was it the cheese? It was really scary.

He picked up the pencil and put it carefully away in the drawer with the secret photo. Stunned by what he had done. He crawled into bed and switched off the light.

꙳

Next morning he was woken up by the sound of the bathroom door banging shut. The drawing was still there on his desk. Mum would be in any minute. He shoved the drawing to the back of his file. Quickly, on the top page, he threw together a simple drawing of a house: a rectangle for a wall, a triangle for a roof and squares for windows. Oh, and a chimney with some smoke coming out. That should ensure some breakfast.

Surprisingly, Mum was in a good mood. When he showed her the baby-like drawing, she just shook her head and shrugged her shoulders.

'Come on get your breakfast; you'll be late for school.'

~

Art was the last lesson of the day. Mr Struthers thought it was a fun lesson to finish on. So Alan had all day to ponder about the drawings. Which one should he hand in. In both cases he was going to get into trouble. His baby-like effort would lead to Mr Struthers talking to his Mum after school, and that would be a week without TV. On the other hand he could give in the magic drawing. But nobody would believe that he could draw like that. They would think he'd pinched it. And if they asked him to show them how he'd done it, he'd never be able to. He couldn't even ask Tony, his best mate, what to do. He was off school with chickenpox. For a brief second he thought of asking Slimy Smith, but instantly dismissed the idea.

Eventually it was time for the art lesson. The first thing Mr Struthers asked them for was the list of places where people lived. Alan groaned. He'd completely forgotten about that bit of the homework. Mr Struthers looked down his nose at him in annoyance as Alan quickly scrawled his list: house, flat, bungalow, igloo... Slimy Smith had the biggest list of course one hundred and twenty seven including, space station and shop doorway.

Then it was the drawing competition. Alan decided he'd nothing to lose. He spread out the magic drawing on his desk and crossed his fingers and toes. Mr Struthers worked his way around the class. Alan breathed a sigh of relief. The teacher wasn't even going to bother looking at his. And then Mr Struthers seemed to realise his mistake. The teacher's eyes popped, and his mouth opened wide. For an instant their eyes met. Without saying anything Mr Struthers turned away and went to the front of the class.

'This week's stars for drawing go to Selina Smith,' and, he paused, 'Alan Jones.'

Alan couldn't believe his ears. He picked up his star in a dream. He was only vaguely aware of the lesson ending and the class being dismissed. He slipped the drawing into his folder and made his way towards the door. But he didn't make it through.

'Alan, I want a word with your Mother. Is she picking you up today?'

He nodded.

'Wait here.'

Alan crumpled in a heap on the side bench. Now they'd want to know where the drawing had come from. This was going to be no telly for a month; maybe no telly ever.

Mr Struthers re-appeared and then, Alan couldn't believe his eyes, his Dad. All thoughts of drawings, stars and blank television screens vanished. He ran and threw his arms around his Dad's waist. Then he noticed his Mum.

'I was keeping it as surprise,' she said.

'So what's this all about?' His Dad said to Mr Struthers.

'Alan, show your Dad your drawing.'

Reluctantly he pulled it out of the file and handed it over

'Wow,' said his Dad.

'Gosh,' said his Mum. 'Did you do that?'

'Well I...' But he never got the chance to say that it had happened by magic.

'Of course he did,' said Mr Struthers. Alan listened in amazement.

'I've been waiting all year for Alan to show me what he could do. This is a beautiful technical drawing, just look at the detail of the pumps and pipelines on the oilrig platform. He doodles in his other lessons.' Mr Struthers routed through a stack of exercise books. 'Look at these.'

Alan squirmed as the teacher showed his Mum and Dad the lovely illustrations of his work that filled the margins of every page. He bit his lip. He just hadn't realised he'd been doing it.

'I just wanted to let you know what a wonderful improvement Alan has made this term,' said Mr Struthers. 'And it is nice to see you back safe and sound from the oilrigs Mr Jones. Are you having a long break this time?'

'Very long. I start a shore based job at the refinery down the road, straight after we've had a holiday.'

Alan floated home, his Mum holding one hand and his Dad the other. And when they went into the house his Mum closed the door - quietly.

Peter Scarisbrick
Compromise

A solidly built man with a bright red, hedgehog hairstyle came into the room, sporting black leather trousers, a studded jacket and heavy, black biker boots. Nelly, the Chair of the Parish Council, had never seen anyone less like a vicar. Surely there must be some mistake. The Bishop couldn't possibly expect the genteel Parish of Saint Pauls to accept this… this creature as their new vicar. Nelly was in fact so shocked that she forgot to invite the candidate to sit down.

'Reverend-' she checked her notes, 'Wellbeloved,' she said, forcing a smile onto her face.

The candidate smiled back and confidently pulled out the interview chair. Then he proceeded to command the space by turning the chair to one side, sitting down and stretching out his long legs.

Nelly turned to the other two members of the interview panel. 'This is the Reverend Wellbeloved,' she said, vacuously, playing for time to gather her thoughts. She was aware that Robin and Malcolm were just as shocked. Luckily she could afford to be diplomatic; there were two other candidates to interview after this one.

'You're not quite what we were expecting,' she said. 'But I am sure you have a wealth of experience. Can you tell us about your previous Ministries?'

When he answered; Nelly nearly fainted. It wasn't what he said, but the fact that as he said it the ball bearing stud in his tongue became visible.

'For the last ten years I've been Chaplain to the Hell's Angels. I have travelled far and wide and have very much enjoyed bringing the message of Christ to the young and not so young members of this special community. Now, I want to have a parish base from which I can continue my work. I will of course dedicate myself to the wonderful rural parish of Saint Paul's and all the people who live here. I would very much like to invite my friends in the biking community to come and visit us. As a thriving Christian community we would be able to show them the love of God and the fellowship of the Holy Spirit. Perhaps some of the more adventurous, and the leaders of the community - like yourselves would be inspired to come with me when I visit them. When you get to know these people you will love them. You wouldn't need a motor bike. I have a two-seater Harley and I can even attach a sidecar.'

Nelly, afterwards, could hardly remember how she got through the rest of the interview. She was vaguely aware that it was the candidate who was supposed to be stressed and nervous. But somehow the Reverend Wellbeloved looked angelically calm throughout the proceedings, while she felt more and more threatened. As he closed the door behind him Nelly felt a bead of sweat run down the back of her neck. Malcolm looked at her. Then in unison they shook their heads.

Nelly looked down at her meagre notes; there were just three names. Why hadn't the Bishop sent the CVs ahead. It was so remiss of him and he was usually so efficient. The next candidate was 'The Reverend Holden'. Neither of the two remaining candidates had arrived before they had started the first interview. Nelly waited awhile to give time for the Reverend Wellbeloved to be well gone before she went out to invite in the next candidate.

There were two people sitting on the bench outside the interview room, a tall, bald-headed man in a grey suit and dog collar, and sitting next to him a woman in a flowery dress. Nelly's first reaction was caution. Why would a candidate bring his wife along with him? Perhaps she wanted to see the parish - perhaps she would have the final say in whether he accepted the job. She hoped that the woman wasn't thinking she could be included in the interview.

'Reverend Holden,' she called.

For the second time that day, Nelly was taken aback. The woman in the flowery dress got up and came towards her, hand outstretched.

'I'm so glad to meet you,' she said. What a lovely parish you have, stunningly beautiful, all spring flowers out on the village green and a tea shop to die for. And the church of Saint Pauls is just wonderful, the Portland stone and the Saxon spire. You're so lucky.'

The Reverend Holden was still gushing about the village as Nelly led her into the interview room. While she was facing away from the candidate, she lifted her eyebrows high towards her colleagues. 'Robin and Malcolm, this is the Reverend Holden.'

'Please, call me Daisy,' said the Reverend Holden.

Nelly had a feeling of deja-vue as she said. 'You're not quite what we were expecting, Reverend Holden.'

'Why ever not?' Daisy replied with a disarming smile. 'You weren't expecting a man, were you?' She went on. 'I know some people can't get on with women vicars, but honestly we can do the job just as well as our male colleagues, and I know I shouldn't say this, but at stressful times when parishioners need a shoulder to cry on, I think women vicars steal a march on the menfolk.'

Again, Nelly was caught up in her own thoughts throughout the interview. Luckily Robin and Malcolm kept the ball rolling. How much experience had the Reverend Holden had? Why did she want to leave her old parish? How did she see herself as 'Vicar of Saint Pauls'?

But the only person Nelly could think about was the old Reverend Brown. He had relied on her, tried out his sermons on her, taken her guidance about decorating the church and managing the graveyard. This Daisy woman wouldn't want her advice. She would have her own ideas. No, a woman vicar was unthinkable. They still had one more candidate to see, the man she'd seen outside.

The interview came to an end and Nelly thanked the Reverend Holden and assured her that they would make a quick decision and relay their recommendation to the Bishop. But it was only fair that they interviewed all three candidates. As the door shut behind the Reverend Holden, Nelly looked at her colleagues. She shook her head. Robin and Malcolm looked a bit disappointed.

Nelly reminded herself of the third candidate's name, the Reverend Ostwald. A minute or two later Nelly led the tall man into the interview room. He sat down on the edge of the chair in a manner that struck Nelly as nervous.

Malcolm got in with the first question. 'What attracts you to the Parish of Saint Pauls?'

'Oh the peace and quiet, just the very fact that it different to my present ministry.'

'Which is?' butted in Nelly.

'Oh, didn't the Bishop tell you - I am the diocesan exorcist. I have been casting out devils for the last decade. But I am afraid Satan is wearing me down, and I am looking for a place of rest. I am obliged to tell you however that I am not a well man. The toll of decades of exorcisms has left my mind fragile and my soul troubled. I am fearful that the Devil may seek me out to extract his revenge upon me wherever I may go. I am sure however that this restful, rural, retreat of a parish is just the place for me. But I am fearful that Satan would delight in bringing death and destruction to such an idyll. I am sure though with all our combined prayers we can hold Satan at bay and live happily to the end of our days.'

All Nelly could think about was *'Ghostbusters'* - a film, which many years ago, against her better judgement, she had taken her children to see. And here was a vicar, a man of God, convinced that he was Bill Murray.

By the time the Reverend Ostwald left, Nelly was very confused and very annoyed. There wasn't one suitable candidate. A long talk with Robin and Malcolm proved fruitless. She was convinced they had both gone doe-eyed over Daisy. She had never felt any pressure, in the past, being the Chair of the Parish Council, but now she was acutely aware that their choice was going to be far reaching for the parish and the village. She even thought of ringing the Bishop and asking for alternative candidates. But the rules were very clear. The candidate will be recommended to the Bishop from a shortlist of three. In the end Robin and Malcolm bottled out. She didn't know how they did it but she was sure that they had colluded. Robin went for Wellbeloved; Malcolm went for Ostwald and that left Nelly with the Chair's deciding vote. Whoever she wanted would be the Parish Councils recommendation. Nelly decided to sleep on it and phone the Bishop the next morning.

༶

At precisely ten thirty she made the call. The Bishop looked pleased as he put down the phone at the end of the conversation. He turned to his Chief Exorcist and his Hells Angels Chaplain with whom he was having morning coffee.

'That was Nelly Nobel on the phone. The Parish have recommended the Reverend Holden. Thank you so much for your help yesterday. I knew they would go for the compromise candidate. I think we may yet meet our quota for parishes in the diocese run by women vicars.'

Peter Scarisbrick
Lawrence (of Arabia)

Lawrence collapsed to his knees, coughing as his throat closed. Now the sand was burning his shins as well as the soles of his feet. Ahead was another dune, white and blinding. The sun was directly overhead and the shade from his straw hat was non-existent. Earlier he had been sweating but now he was bone dry, every drop of moisture baked out. Even his eyes hurt, gritty and shrunken from the drying out of the aqueous humour. How had he been so stupid. He tried to stand, but the sand shifted under him. He so wanted to lie down, but he knew the sun would fry him even more quickly. Perhaps that would be better.

Even though his eyes were now closed he could see the sun through his eyelids, not yellow, not red, but a blazing blue-white orb that drifted around in his head erasing his memories. And then there was this net, sail-like, sweeping up his thoughts, dragging them away. Soon he was conscious only of a blinding light that filled his mind completely.

Then in an instant the sun disappeared. A cool breeze hit him like a winter storm. He shivered and opened his eyes. Towering above him and holding out an ice cream, his wife looked down at him in his deckchair.

'You shouldn't sleep in the sun, you know - you'll get a migraine.'

Christine Milliken
An Organised Affair - An Alternative Fairytale

He leant his folded arms upon the delicate, scroll-worked, iron railing and his eyes gazed unseeing on the vast ballroom below. All was quiet now; just a lone maidservant polishing an ornate vase, which rested on a plinth in a small recess. He wished it could always be like this. He hated grand occasions; he preferred the company of close friends to the fawning pretences of his father's courtiers.

He heard footsteps approaching along the gallery behind him. He groaned and wondered what else could possibly require his attention. A most un-servant like slap on the back, accompanied by a cheerful greeting, jolted him around. His best friend, Velcro, was dark, tall and what the ladies regarded as handsome. He stood in front of Prince Alluring grinning and bouncing from foot to foot with impatience.

'Come on, I've got something for you,' he said. He clearly did not expect arguments from his prince and turned around and headed back the way he had come. Alluring glanced once more at the ballroom beneath him, then set off after his friend.

'Your Highness!' a voice called from further along the apparently never-ending hallway. He sighed and then turned to wait for his father's steward to come panting toward him, a large folder held ominously in his hands. Velcro turned back, gave Alluring a sympathetic look and then shrugged, before continuing on his way leaving him once again to face the trials of his elevated position. How Alluring so envied the carefree existence of Velcro.

'My lord,' the elderly retainer almost pleaded. 'We must go over the final arrangements for tonight.'

Alluring sighed once more. There would be no merry escapade with Velcro today. Indeed, if his parents had their way, their friendship would be over for good.

܀

Hundreds of candles flickered in chandeliers and sconces, lighting the ballroom with a magical glow, sparkling on the jewels and sequins which adorned both women and men as they danced in time to the music floating down from the Minstrels' Gallery. Sitting on his own throne beside his mother and father, Alluring stared out at the couples dancing gracefully around the room. Groups of older people stood, or were seated around the perimeter; some were laughing, others intent on the couples dancing and he could see others glancing surreptitiously in his direction before continuing their conversations. He knew he was scowling and didn't try to hide it. Another group moved toward the dais, the man bowed and then introduced his family; yet another minor noble, with two rather plain daughters who curtsied while peeping through their eyelashes at him. The elder winked at him and he felt his cheeks redden. Damn all these people. This was not how it was supposed to be. At last they retreated.

The music changed to a waltz and he was pleased to see Velcro approaching, a handsome, if not quite beautiful, young woman hanging upon his arm. Quickly, he rose to join them before his father could call him back. They sidestepped around the couples on the dance floor, although that was not really necessary as the dancers hurried to make way for the young prince. At last, laughing, they raced through the great marble doors out into the clear, crisp night air and Alluring's life changed forever.

She sat on the broad palace steps. As she leaned forward to adjust the straps of her crystal, high heeled shoes, she seemed to be engulfed by fountains of silk and lace. Straightening, from her task she saw him watching her.

'Well, are you going to stand there all day like a scarecrow, or are you going to give me a hand up?' She stared at him without any sign of meekness, her arm held out waiting for his aid.

He rushed to her side and helped her to her feet. No one spoke to him like that; although her harsh words had been softened by her gentle, melodious voice. Then she smiled at him, an impish grin. His heart pounded against his chest and his blood raced around his body.

'We were just going down to the lake,' he said. 'Would you care to join us?'

She looked up toward the lights and music which escaped from the palace, then back to him and to his amazement, she laughed and grabbed his hand and ran down the steps. 'Who wants to meet some stuffy old prince, anyhow,' she laughed. And he laughed too.

☙

They twirled around the dance floor, oblivious to all else in the room. Young women and their mothers glowered in disgust. What a waste of time it had been, the prince had been missing for most of the evening and on his return remained inseparable from the raven-haired girl who no one seemed to know.

As the evening drew on Alluring danced as if in a trance. He was utterly enchanted by her beauty, poise and honest normality. He determined that any objections would be overcome. He had found his other half, he knew she was the one who would fill the chasm within him and make him whole at last.

The clock struck midnight and the musicians paused. She carefully untangled his arms from around her and leant up and kissed him on the cheek. Then she turned and ran from the room.

He stood and watched as she glided gracefully away, drinking in the motion of her body, wrapped by swirling lace. Suddenly he seemed to awake as if from a dream. She had gone! He had stood and watched her leave! He didn't even know her name.

He ran out into the cool night. There was no one to be seen. He sank down forlornly on to the topmost step and bent his head in grief, his elbows resting on his knees, his hands over his eyes.

So it was that Velcro found him. Concern for his best friend was overtaken by a desire to help him however he could. He searched around in the glimmering torchlight for a clue, anything to tell him where she had gone. Finally, when he had almost given up hope, he found a sign, a token of her passing. Returning to his friend he laid the offering carefully on Alluring's knee. Alluring stared at the strange object. It was clear, oval-shaped and made of a gel-like substance. 'I don't understand' he groaned. 'What is it? How will it help me find her?'

Velcro was a man of the world, unlike his friend who lived within the confines of the royal palace. 'It is what women wear inside their shoes,' he explained, 'so they can dance all night in those high heels.' Alluring looked at the strange item in amazement. He was touching where her foot had been. As he turned it over in his hands he was thrilled to be holding something so personal to her.

'But how does it help us find her?' he asked in bewilderment.

'That, my friend,' Velcro replied, 'is where the wonder of technology steps in. Excuse the pun! Her unique foot print is now etched into the gel and from that we can make a model of her foot.' Alluring still looked puzzled, so his friend continued, 'And then we just have to find whoever it matches with and you will have found her.'

And so it happened. Alluring entrusted his best friend with the task of locating his love. A model was made and Velcro set out with a troop of the King's guardsmen. He scoured the kingdom, visiting all the gentry, the wealthy business men and families of standing, but to no avail. In his absence, the prince remained in his apartments, refusing food, speaking to no-one, his only companion a small gel in-step. His parents, the King and Queen grew increasingly concerned. Doctors were summoned, nutritionists counselled, but nothing they could do was of any help.

At last Velcro returned. The soldiers were tired and hungry. Their quest had failed. The King drew himself up, in all his stately grandeur, 'This will not do,' he proclaimed. 'The maiden must be found. Velcro, go forth again! Search every house, every homestead. The girl must be found!' So Velcro set out once more. This time he vowed to visit every house in the land until he found his best friend's love.

Thus it was, that at last, on a cool Autumn day, he arrived at the village of Far Out Land and as he came to the last house, his search was finally over. In the kitchen he found the one he sought. Her raven hair fell over her face as she bent down to place her foot inside the cast. The fit was perfect.

'Bloomin' 'eck,' she cried, 'It's a perfect fit.' Velcro lifted her in his arms and took her out to the waiting men. They cheered and clapped as he placed her on his own horse and then mounted behind her. It was a very merry group which cantered back to the palace that night.

Alluring was curled up on the chair, close by the fire, lost in his own thoughts and gripping tightly to his only token of his lost love, when Velcro burst into the room and unceremoniously dumped the girl upon his lap.

'Velcro, is this some kind of joke?' he spluttered, enraged. Then, as he looked down into the wells of her eyes, all anger died.

'Whatever is going on?' she demanded. 'First, this idiot grabs me from my home, then he flings me on his smelly, old horse and we ride half across the country and then he dumps me in here. Who are you anyway?' Her blustering bravado died and she gazed shyly into his eyes.

Velcro stepped forward and bowed formally. 'May I introduce His Royal Highness, The Prince Alluring.' He flourished another bow for good measure. 'And Your Royal Highness, I should like to present...' He looked enquiringly at the girl who seemed to be quite comfortably seated on her prince's knee. 'Madam, I fear I do not know your name.'

'It's Ash,' she said, 'short for Asherella. You can call me Ash.'

And so it was, the prince had found his Ash. And as all good fairy tales end, nothing remains but to say Alluring married his Ash and they lived happily ever after.

The End

Christine Milliken

Forbidden Love - an old-fashioned Love Story

His hands gently pulled free of her wavy tresses. He surveyed his handywork and grinned impishly at the sight of the buttercups and meadowsweet intertwined amid her golden locks. As she lay down amongst the sweet-smelling flowers, he thought she was the most beautiful person he had ever seen. She laughed up at him and pulled him down next to her. He wished this moment could last forever. The light was fading and he knew it was time to see her safely home as he had done every night for the last six weeks of the summer.

The shadows, cast by the trees which lined the aptly named 'Cherry Tree Lane' had lengthened and enveloped the road with their gloom as the young couple clung to each other in a last embrace. Finally they untangled their arms and he watched as she crossed the road and opened the gate which led to her home. As the door opened she was immersed in a pool of light, but too soon the door closed and the darkness seeped into his being. He wistfully imagined being invited inside; there would be a handshake from her father and an offer of tea from her mother, they would sit and chat about their lives and plans for the future. He sighed, turned and retraced his steps out of the village.

'Suzanne, you are a complete mess.' Her mother accosted her before she had a chance to escape upstairs to her room. 'For heaven's sake, girl. What have you been doing? There are grass stains on your blouse – and what is that caught in your hair?'

Suzanne shrugged, 'Sorry Mum. Pauline and I went down to the river as it was such a nice day. I fell asleep on the riverbank.'

'Didn't your father tell you to stay in the village? You really shouldn't be wandering the countryside, not with those gypsies camped over the other side of the valley. You can't be too careful.'

'Sorry Mum,' she answered. 'I'll stay in the village from now on.' She hastily continued up the stairs before her mother could question her further. She had always been sensible and obedient and she wasn't used to telling lies to her parents, but she could hardly tell them the truth!

As she sat at her dressing table, she carefully removed the wilting flowers. She brushed her hair, removing a few stray grass stems and a tiny bright green caterpillar that had crawled into her hair. She gently placed it on a leaf of ivy which grew outside her window. She breathed in the smells of the outdoors. She could almost imagine the sweet perfume of the wild flower meadow and beyond that the smoky smell of a camp fire. She thought of his unruly, black, curly hair and his dark, piercing eyes which seemed to peer right into her soul. What was he doing now?

☙

His attempt at a quiet entry into the camp was thwarted by the joyful barking of Dodger, who raced to greet him, his tail wagging as he jumped up at him.

'Down boy!' Anton knelt to hug the shaggy mongrel who was licking his face enthusiastically. Had the dog caught her unfamiliar scent which lingered on him? The rumpus alerted his mother to his arrival and she soon had him busy helping her with preparations for the evening meal. She wondered at the grin on his face and laughter in his eyes. Theirs wasn't an easy life, especially for a teenage boy, so whatever or whoever had given her son cause to smile had her approval.

The screeching of brakes and tyres attempting to gain grip on the muddy field, heralded the arrival of his father and uncles in their Ford Anglia van, returning from their day's labours.

'Anton,' his mother whispered to him. 'You'd best get rid of that grin, you know how suspicious your father can be at anything out of the ordinary.' With an effort he reverted to his usual sour look which he wore in the presence of his father.

Having the typical swarthy features of the true Romany, Anton's father swept into the campsite and disappeared into their caravan home. By the time he re-emerged, washed and his hair neatly brushed, the steaming stew was poured on to the plates. The next few minutes were given over to the serious business of eating, but then his father sat back on his chair and lit his ancient pipe. As he puffed, the aromatic, woody scents of tobacco engulfed them. He looked at his son.

'Well, Anton, what have you been doing today?' he asked.

'Just the usual,' Anton answered. 'I went down to the river. I think I'll take my rod tomorrow and see what I can catch.' His father nodded his approval.

Later that night, as Anton lay down in his tiny but neat bedroom, he thought back over his day and especially remembered the golden-haired girl. Outside he could hear his parents talking. Snatches of conversation hinting at trouble with magistrates, threats of bailiffs and police. He sighed and returned to his own thoughts.

༄

Anton arrived early at the meadow by the gently flowing river. A water vole scurried to the shelter of its hole. A pair of ducks paddled in the shallows, heads dipping below the surface as they rummaged for grubs, snowy white plumage broadcasting their Aylesbury heritage. A dragonfly flitted among the tall water reeds, its brilliant blue body and wings translucent in the early morning rays. Anton settled himself down on the bank and busied himself preparing his fishing rod and then he cast it far out across the river. It landed with a plop and ripples radiated outward where it entered the previously still water. He lay down and let the sun's rays warm his body. Soon he fell asleep. The riverbank creatures ignored him and continued with their business, unaffected by the world beyond their own small domain.

A tugging of the rod, which rested loosely on his palm, brought him to sudden wakefulness. He stood up and pulled in the line. A gleaming, silver fish dangled, trapped on the hook. He brought it to land and quickly ended its agonised gasps for breath with a firm slap on a small rock.

His sleepy idleness over, he hastened to gather twigs and soon had a small fire blazing on the sandy riverside. Expertly he gutted and washed the fish and placed it on the now glowing embers of his fire. He sat back, pleased with his work and only then noticed that the sun was now high in the sky. He had slept longer than he had thought. Where was she? Why hadn't she come? He carefully turned the fish, then he strolled across the meadow to the lane beyond. There was no one to be seen on the road which led south to the village.

Voices coming from the opposite direction alerted him to the approaching group of women coming down the river from the camp. He ducked down behind the hawthorn bushes which lined the road. Laughing and chattering, the rich sounds of the Romany language passed by and then faded into the distance as the women went to the village laden with bunches of lavender and homemade wooden pegs.

Anton returned to his small fire, but the fish was charred and his hunger vanished with the sun which retreated behind a bank of cumulus clouds. He kicked sand over the remains of the fire, dowsing the last flames. Then he set off across the field, scrambling through the gap in the hedge and headed south down the lane, being careful that his long strides didn't catch up with the group of women ambling merrily along in front.

Cherry Tree Road was situated in what was considered a 'desirable location'. Houses were in great demand. Few came on the market as no one wanted to leave. Those that did went in pursuit of career and wealth in the city, while those that stayed behind thought they had made the better choice. But today, things were changing at a pace unseen in the village for years. There was outrage and demands for action. People, who rarely spoke, now talked as if old friends, united in their desire to rid their village of the gypsy camp. A group of locals were massed outside the village store, jostling to have their opinions heard; while Sergeant Martins, the local bobby, nodded and muttered his agreement, while hoping he would not be the one required to visit the camp.

It was into this bustle that the gypsy women arrived. Seeing a group of potential customers gathered together, they hurried over to join them.

By the time Anton arrived, the two groups had become a seething mass of shouting and angry residents and bewildered, while equally vociferous gypsy women. Giving a wide berth to the feuding parties, Anton hurried on down the street until he reached Suzanne's house.

The family's blue Cortina was parked in the drive, a sure sign that Suzanne's father was home. Anton slipped into the lane at the side of the house and crept around to the back garden. The French windows were flung wide to let in the fresh, summer air. A man's voice was raised in anger. Anton listened with rising dread. 'How can we ever trust you again?' it demanded. "You have brought shame on this whole family.' Anton thought he heard soft crying. His heart breaking inside him, he crept closer to the open doors.

Suzanne's father was in full flow now. 'Dirt sticks, you know - and you're as 'muddy as a bog in winter!' If your mother hadn't met Mrs Peters and found out that Pauline had been in bed with flu all week, I imagine you'd be out there right now, sullying the good name of this family.'

Anton backed away. What was the point in staying? Suzanne would never be allowed to see him again. Reluctantly, he retreated out of the village and took the lane back to his own home. He doubted he would ever see her again.

It had been an unpleasant two weeks. Bailiffs had arrived at the camp, accompanied by reporters and cameramen representing the local TV company. Voices had been raised. A camera broken. A fight had ensued, resulting in Anton's father and uncles being arrested. They had eventually been released, but only after payment of a hundred pound fine and assurance that they would leave the area and not return. So now an air of gloom pervaded the camp as once more, belongings were stowed away and the small community prepared to travel again.

Anton went down to the river one final time. The heaviness in his heart was not even lifted by the sight of the ducks, who had overcome their shyness of him, and now proudly paraded their seven, yellow downy ducklings for him to inspect. He reached down and selected a small flat pebble. He studied it closely, the smoothness of its water worn surface made him think of how he had changed these last few weeks, the roughness rubbed off him by knowing Suzanne. He held it carefully, like a discus, then threw it, spinning out in a shallow arc over the water, until it landed with four skimming splashes in the far reaches of the river. He sighed and turned away with a heavy heart to return to his people.

It was then he saw her. She was standing in the shade of the old horse chestnut tree, watching him. She smiled and then ran toward him. At first he just stood and watched her, convinced that his desires had conjured up a phantom to deceive him, but as she drew near, he too began to run and they were soon wrapped in each other's arms. They fell to the ground overwhelmed by their delight at being together again.

It was some time before he came to his senses and pulled away from her. She stared up at him quizzically, perplexed by his serious expression. 'I'm leaving tonight. We have to move on.' he said.

Her earnest blue eyes gazed into his. 'I know, she replied. "I'm coming too.' It was only then that he noticed the small holdall which she had flung to the ground.

The last rays of the setting sun streaked across the sky. Swifts swirled in endless flight. A rustling in the reeds at the water's edge heralded the waking of the nocturnal river animals. The last of the gaily-painted caravans was hauled out of the ruts in the little lane and the procession wound its way west toward the setting sun.

The village regained its sleepy demeanour, soft orange lights glimmering through the windows, cats prowling for mice. A family of badgers crept on to a lawn to feast on the food provided by the kind-hearted residents. The clock on the church tower chimed half past ten.

Four miles north of the village, two shadowy figures made a small camp for the night. What the future held, they didn't know, but for now, for this night, they were together.

John Edwards
Life's Full of Surprises

One day in the summer holidays, me and a few of the gang were bored and sitting on the pavement at the top of our road. We were guessing the names of cars as they approached in the distance. Albie Fletcher was best at this.

'Sunbeam Talbot,' he said before any of us could see it clearly. And it was.

The day before we had been playing soccer in the school playground but Wacca Walker the caretaker had copped us and chased us off. That meant soccer was off the agenda. Jimmy Thompson and Dolly Dolman suggested we split up and go knocking on doors to scrounge any old rags or pop bottles. Pop bottles fetched a penny apiece at Rutters wine shop and if we got enough old rags or woollens we could knock up two bob between us from Joe Bell's scrap yard. Me and Albie got Cambridge Road, Wellington Road and Cromwell Road. Jimmy and Dolly Dolman got Kingsley Road, Exeter Road and Holly Road. Then we split up and off we went.

I said to Albie, 'You do this side and I'll do the other,'

'OK', said Albie, 'but don't knock on number ten down there, it's Sam Rich's. He's a miserable bugger an' he'll probably give you a thick ear.'

We had agreed to meet on the old derelict patch behind the Phoenix Club at two o' clock. After having no luck at the first half a dozen houses, I shouted across to Albie, 'Blimey, we won't get rich at this rate.'

'Oh I don't know, I got a bag of rags off old man Geary and two empty pop bottles from Mrs Gibbons,' he gloated.

'Wow, you lucky dog, still, maybe up the road I'll do better,' I said hopefully.

At number fourteen I lifted the brass door knocker and rather strangely the door opened slightly. I asked if anyone was there, but got no reply. I looked down the dark lobby where bare, brown walls contrasted with the shiny lino on the floor. I called several times but there was still no answer. Albie was across the street, shoving his rags into an old sack he'd nicked from the station coal yard. I called to him that something seemed a bit strange. Mrs Phibbs never left her door open as a rule and I was suddenly filled with concern. She was a lovely old lady and she would often reach into her deep, leather shopping bag and produce a sherbet lolly for us when we were playing *tip-it-and-run*, in the street.

I pushed the door open a bit more and crept along the lobby. I knocked on the front room door. Nothing. I moved along to the back room door and it was slightly ajar. Then, I could hear a moaning sound which scared me out of my wits. I didn't fancy running into any ghosts.

'Hello, Mrs Phibbs, are you OK?' I said tentatively. She looked up.

'Oh, thank God, please go and get Mrs Farren from next door to help me.'

I ran down the lobby like Macdonald Bailey and hammered on the big knocker on the house next door Mrs Farren opened the door a little to see what the racket was all about. When she saw me she asked what was going on. I could hardly get the words out as I spluttered and gulped and told her about poor Mrs Phibbs.

'Right, good lad,' said Mrs Farren as she patted my head with her large, washerwoman hand, which almost sent me reeling. She went next door to help Mrs Phibbs up onto the sofa and asked Mr Farren to phone for an ambulance.

When the ambulance arrived the whole street turned out to watch. Standing in small groups, each with a different version of events. I ran round full of importance telling that it was me who had found her and got Mrs Farren too. When the ambulance had gone, peace was restored and the groups broke up and went back inside their homes.

Me and Albie sat on the pavement, as usual, and when Mr Gibbons strolled past, I asked him what the time was. He told us it was half past one as he studied the large fob watch from his waistcoat. Albie was grumbling that all the fuss and bother with Mrs Phibbs had held us up from our important task.

'Bet the others have got loads more than us, they'll think we've been skiving.' he said. So we legged it round to the patch to meet up with them.

We'd just turned out of Holly Road when a man called to us from across the road. It was Arthur, Mrs Phibb's son. We'd seen him going to visit his mother many times. I told Albie to get ready to run in case he told us off for going into his mother's house. However, he came across the road and stood in front of us.

'Listen Mr Phibbs, I wasn't doin' anything wrong you know. I was just knocking to collect rags and when the door opened I thought it seemed a bit strange. I wasn't nickin' stuff, honest.'

'It's OK, son, calm down. I just wanted to thank you. Me Mam could have been lying there all day and night but for you.' Then he patted me on the head and reached into his pocket. He pressed a half crown in my hand and went on his way.

I looked at Albie with a huge grin on my face. 'Crikey,' I said, 'I thought I'd get nothing today!' Ain't life full of surprises.

John Edwards
Memories

At one end of the old, terraced street where I was born stands a large, red-brick Infants and Junior school with a big playground. Standing here, looking over the wall into the playground as the sun is low in the sky, memories of my childhood come flooding into my mind.

My ears are suddenly ringing with the cacophony of sounds of children playing, running, shouting, and laughing. The names of the kids in my class, I can't remember them all, just a few, but I can see their faces, and almost hear their voices.

❧

The school was very close to our house so I was always early, usually running around the playground, playing *tick*, football or just throwing an old tennis ball against the wall and catching it.

My teacher in the final year was Mr Breakwell, a big man, a tough disciplinarian, but a man who loved poetry. He would ask different kids to come out to the front of the class to recite poetry. If he thought they had read well he would give them a threepenny piece. My favourite poem was '*Sea Fever*' by John Masefield and I had memorised it so that I didn't need to read from the book. Threepence to me, then, was a small fortune, so I practised and polished my performance at home, spurred on by the thought of a Cowans toffee bar or a bag of aniseed balls after school.

The thought came into my mind that the rough and tumble camaraderie and spirit of that school came from the fact that we were all more or less from the same poor families, but there was nothing to make us realise how poor we were. In 1952, life was still recovering from the war, and elements of our play still included running round with outstretched arms believing we were heroic Spitfire pilots shooting down the enemy.

༄

I turn away from the school with my eyes moistened by memories and look down to the end of our street with fifteen terraced houses on each side. Into my mind's eye comes a picture of my mother, kneeling at the front step, whitening the edge of it with a stepstone, a bucket of steaming water at her elbow. I can hear her saying to me, 'No, you can't come in yet, you'll have to go round the back way'.

As I look to the other end of the street, I see the dark, corrugated iron buildings of the large steel fabrication factory where I was to work eventually, but that was after a journey which took me away from my home town for the first time in the whole of my eleven years. Not completely away, but away enough.

I passed the 11 plus exam. The family line for outside consumption in our road was, 'Our John's passed his scholarship.' No other kid in the street had. Inside the home though, the pride was severely diluted with the talk being of how my parents were going to afford the expense. The purchasing of the school uniform and all the extras that went with it loomed over the whole household as a huge worry.

In those days we boys wore boots because they lasted longer than shoes. Despite my desperate pleas, and even secret plans to run away, I was sent to Wirral Grammar School in black, shiny boots with black tags on the back.

For the first time in my life, and for a long time to come, I was made to realise how poor we really were and what humiliation at the hands of others felt like. I was the only boy wearing boots.

How I longed to go back and recite, 'Sea Fever,' for Mr Breakwell.

John Edwards
We Nearly Got Rich

Me and Jimmy Thompson were sitting on the pavement in Holly Road. We were counting our marbles and comparing and showing off the best we had. Both of us knew where we got our swaps and where we won the others. It was a matter of great pride when you won a *'tor'*, as we called the most colourful marbles.

It was mid-December and there was a biting chill in the wind. Jimmy was lucky enough to have a woolly hat and he pulled it down. I pulled my collar up and wiped my nose on my sleeve. Jimmy asked what I was getting for Christmas, but I said I didn't know. I told him I'd seen a smashing fort and soldiers in Gavagan's window and I almost trembled when I thought how much I would have cherished it. There was also a casey ball and some footy boots which I had looked at longingly. When I told Jimmy about them, he was disbelieving and said we'd all be lucky to get a bag of sweets and *The Beano* or the *Dandy* annual. I knew he was right. We both remembered Ray Thomas getting a bike for last Christmas and he wouldn't even let us touch it.

Just then, I was called into the house. Me Mam wanted me to run an errand for her. I had to go to Joe Hughes' shop for a quarter of butter and three eggs, with strict instructions not to break any of them, under pain of death!

Jimmy and me put our marbles in our special safe place then he came to the shop with me. We played at no treading on the cracks in the pavement and were nearly falling over each other when a breeze swept along the street. Suddenly out of nowhere, coming towards us, floating on the wind, right in front of us was a ten bob note. There wasn't a soul in sight. We both looked left then right a dozen times before Jimmy swooped down and scooped up the note. Then we ran into the entry between Cambo Road School and the shops. We examined the money carefully as if it would disappear before our very eyes, then made a plan. I had to do the errand I had been sent on before we found the riches then we would meet up on the school roof for a *pow-wow*.

I went into Joe Hughes' shop which always smelt of newspapers and tobacco, but at the back of the shop was a cold room with a thick marble counter. On this stood a large, red bacon slicing machine and a large board with a massive block of butter on it. Next to the butter was a slicing knife and wooden paddles for patting it.

I asked for the butter and eggs and watched, as I always did, as he shaped the butter and popped it onto a piece of greaseproof paper on the scales. He put the eggs in a brown paper bag and said the charge was eleven pence. I passed over me Mam's shilling and got the penny change.

When I got home with the things Mam wanted, she gave me a telling-off for taking so long. It was wash-day and the house was full of steam and the smell of Sunlight soap. It wasn't necessary for me to hang around, so Mam just nodded when I told her we were off for a game of footy. Which was a bit if a lie.

At the end of our street was Cambridge Road School and we had our den up on the threepenny-bit roof. We called it that because of its shape. We'd shin up the drain pipe and onto the roof from there. All our important gang meetings were carried out up there. Jimmy and me made our way there with great purpose.

However, on our way we saw Pete Windsor and he was running and out of breath.

'Hey, where's the fire?' we asked him.

Then it all came spilling out. He was in terrible trouble. He had been sent to pick up his Mam's groceries from Mansells at the top of Cambo Road and when he got there he couldn't find the ten bob note she'd given him to pay for them. He was terrified of going home to face his Mam and Dad.

Me and Jimmy looked at each other and we never gave it a second thought. We told Pete our story and gave him the ten bob note. It took him ten minutes to stop sobbing, then he pulled himself together, gave us a watery smile, got his Mam's groceries and went home.

Jimmy and me sat down and made a list of what we would have spent the money on. We nearly got rich.

Annette Hayes
Coffee Time

Mary was rushing. She wanted to get to the coffee shop before the lunch queue. It was her small pleasure, reading the paper in a comfy seat. As she left she would leave the paper for someone else, as if to minimise her guilt for being lazy.

The pain was getting worse, it seared through her. She knew that it was angina. The doctor said to take it easy, but even as a child she was called little Miss Busy. At seventy-five it was too late to change now, she thought as she leant against the shop window pretending to look in. One more pain, worse this time then slowly it ebbed away.

She straightened up and turned, ready to go. Then looking up she caught her breath again. Everything swam in front of her eyes. Sound became muted, somewhere a dog barked, a child was crying, in the distance an ambulance, but far away.

She wasn't sure she had really seen him, but there he was in the Cathedral grounds. John. He was looking at her. He raised two takeaway cups and smiled. She knew she was in some kind of shock, a dry mouth, head swimming, not really the self she knew, but her legs carried her without thinking toward him.

He put the cups down on a bench and called, 'Want me to lift you over?' He was still smiling but she could sense he was nervous. Not surprising after eight years.

Memories flooded back to when they were young. He so tall and her so small and light that he could lift her over the railings with one arm around her waist. In seconds they would both be inside the grounds laughing as they ran to the sunniest spot to sunbathe and talk and talk and talk till it got dark. That was many years ago now.

He was still tall but not quite so upright, and as for her, she could not even step over the cat without difficulty, but she smiled as she shook her head and came through the gate.

'I didn't expect you, a bit of a shock,' she said. Then for something to say as she took the coffee, she nodded to the cup. 'How did you know I was going for coffee?'

'You're a creature of habit.'

'You follow me?' she said, startled.

'No, I see you. Not often…occasionally.'

'Do you see the children?'

'Sometimes, again not often,' he said. 'I saw Jess at the wedding, she looked beautiful'. He wanted to tell her he had seen her too and that she also looked beautiful, but he didn't want to frighten her off.

'I was angry that day,' she said, '- with you.'

'I know.'

The memory made the hurt come back. 'You left me,' she said, then added, 'Us. We needed you, and you just disappeared off like we didn't matter. A month before the wedding. How could you do that?'

She waited for the pain in her chest again, and took some deep breaths but it didn't come this time.

'Have you forgiven me now?' he said.

She suddenly saw the absurdity of it all and laughed. 'Well I don't sound like I have, do I? But I stopped ranting at the empty rooms about four years ago after the crying and the anger all became too tiring.' She looked into his eyes and they returned her gaze with compassion. Then she said, quietly, 'After that I just missed you!'

It felt cruel being angry with him. It wasn't his fault. 'I am only just getting used to you not being there. Finally, I have it in my head that half a dozen eggs will last me a fortnight, although the papers say we can have more of them now. Oh dear, I'm nervous, I'm prattling.'

'It's nice to hear your voice' he said.

'You're very calm. You weren't always so calm, How are you, in yourself I mean?' she asked.

'I'm fine. Well, now I am. At first I had to work out that maybe there's not much point in being anything else but calm, wherever you are.'

'So you didn't miss us then?' She said with a slight ache in her voice.

He sighed. 'I didn't want to go you know. It wasn't like I had a choice, and yes I did miss you and I did have to get used to the loss like you did. But after a while it becomes a very peaceful life with moments of pure joy, with no pain at all - as I see the ones I love.'

'Rotten timing though,' she said, smiling, 'I bet you cursed at the time.'

'I was too stunned. Who has a heart attack on the day the doctor has told them they are going to live to a hundred? I should have sued him. I saw him at the wedding too, drinking my brandy. I knew I should never believe my brother was a real doctor. Heart specialist my eye. There he was telling everyone that it was a complete fluke. At least he had the decency to look guilty.'

'He had a terrible time after you died; I think he really did feel as though he should have been able to predict it.'

Mary was thinking. 'How come you get to see some people and not others?'

He seemed to hesitate, then said, 'That took me a while to work out, but I think I know now. At the wedding, I should have been there and you were all still in shock thinking about me, so I got to be there. Like a connection was made, letting me through.'

'So it was when we thought of you. That makes sense. Jess said she thought you were there, and so did I.' Then she said, 'But today, I wasn't thinking about you at all, I was thinking about coffee and a newspaper and a comfy seat.'

'Yes,' he said. He watched her face as she suddenly realised what was happening. She put her hand over her mouth as if to stop the shock.

Then she said, 'The ambulance I heard, it was for me! And you, you've come for me?' He didn't say anything immediately, watching her closely as the shock gradually eased from her face. When he did speak his voice was tender.

'I have come for you, but only when you are ready. Take your time.' After a few minutes she looked around her trying to commit everything to memory in case she didn't come back.

'Will we get to come back here sometimes?' she said wistfully.

'Often - if you want,' he said gently. 'Or even just for coffee.'

She looked into his loving face then and realised that for a long time she had been waiting just for this moment.

'Then I'm ready,' she said, smiling nervously, and took his outstretched hand.

Annette Hayes
Payback

Tilly sat down and started going through her household bills, getting more and more depressed. It had all seemed such a good idea when she and Laura decided to take on the lease of the little run-down café on the corner six months ago. They had both been excited and worked tirelessly to get it ready, involving everyone they could think of to help clean, decorate and provide little tables and chairs.

None of the chairs matched, and without the little tablecloths from the market the tables were scratched and a mess, but now it looked clean, welcoming and warm, and just the place for a rest after shopping, or before picking up the children from school. The shiny glass cabinets and displays that had been their major cost had proved worthwhile and the cakes and scones with jam and cream seemed to fly off the shelves. The Little Muffin Café looked like it was going to be a success. But was it making a profit?

It was no good, Tilly thought, she would have to ask Laura for some back pay. She decided to settle the most urgent bills, and talk to Laura tomorrow, then, went into the sitting room to sit with Josh for a while before his bedtime. He was watching some nature programme where, as usual, some creature would eventually tear another one to pieces in order to survive. She wondered briefly if this would happen to her and Laura.

They had agreed when they started the business that they would play to their strengths. Tilly would be in charge of baking, food ordering, and overall operation of the café, while Laura would handle all building and financial matters, and help to run things on a daily basis.

For the first year they also agreed that they would take minimum wage and then see if they could afford to pay themselves more.

But Tilly had to work far more hours to cope with early deliveries and final stock control at night, and Laura was just paying them both for a normal week. Tilly tried asking her mum as often as she could to look after Josh but it still often meant she was at the café at seven with Josh in tow to open up. He inevitably was getting grumpy about it and asked her why Laura didn't open up as she didn't have any kids, but Tilly didn't know why so just said she didn't mind.

Josh said 'I do though.'

☙

The next day Laura seemed a bit distracted but Tilly, thinking of Josh and the bills, waited till there was a lull in customers. When she plucked up the courage it all came blurting out.

'I need to talk to you about money - I mean, what I really mean is, I need more money. I need for the business to pay me what I have worked over and above the normal hours,' she said, breathlessly.

'What do you mean, normal hours,' said Laura, frowning, 'There are no normal hours. We agreed we would both work for a year for minimum wage, and it's only been nine months.'

'I know that,' said Tilly, 'but since business picked up I am coming in at least an hour and a half earlier each day and often staying later to lock up.'

At that point Josh came in and sat in his usual corner to wait for Tilly to finish. He smiled but then looked a bit worried as he sensed the friction in the room. Tilly took him over a sandwich and a milk shake as he opened his books to do his homework.

'You ok mum?' said Josh.

Tilly smiled and ruffled his hair. 'Yuk! Hair gel,' she said.

He laughed and said, 'Yeah well, whose fault is that then?'

After a few minutes she went back to where Laura was sitting.

Tilly had known Laura since they were both at the junior school so knew the conversation was not over. She recognised that 'I have raised myself above you,' look on her face. She suddenly felt very tired.

'You do know that I do the washing of the tablecloths in my own time don't you?' said Laura, and then for emphasis, 'and I had to have a meeting about the new oven you wanted, to see if it would comply with all the regulations.'

Tilly looked across at Josh sitting quietly, but obviously listening. Was she just going to let it go, and get nowhere, did Josh think his Mum was a coward? Laura always was the stronger one in an argument. Perhaps, Tilly thought, that's why we get on so well. Then a voice in her head said 'no you get on because you are friends, and friends talk to each other.'

So in a very clear voice she said 'Sorry Laura, but I think when you went to that meeting I was covering for both of us here, and while I agree you do put the tablecloths in the washing machine, if I remember rightly, WE pay your Mum out of OUR funds to do the ironing.'

Laura bristled and said 'Well I didn't ask you to come in earlier just to get more hours did I?'

Tilly tried but was failing to stay calm. 'Laura,' she said exasperatedly, 'I came in when we realised the business was getting too big for just what we could bake here, we agreed it don't you remember? Someone needed to come in for the early deliveries.'

'Well,' said Laura, 'I didn't think it meant I needed to pay you for doing it!'

At this point Josh got up and went to the back of the shop and through to the kitchen. 'Going to get some water,' he muttered.
Tilly had had enough and could feel her cheeks flushing with anger as she replied.

'You know what, Laura, I didn't think YOU would be paying me; I thought this was OUR business and it was the business that would pay me just the hours that I have worked, but I tell you what, just so you don't have to pay out too much this week, I am taking the week off.'

With that she called out 'Josh come on, we are leaving,' just as he came back into the room.

☙

It was odd over the next few days being so free, and strangely unsettling, but fun too. She and Josh went shopping, and to the cinema, and she had time to cook her Mum a lovely meal in return for all the ones she had made over the months of getting the café up and running.

There were several messages from Laura but as soon as she heard her voice Josh darted across the room and deleted them.

'She was horrid mum, let her sweat,' he said. She wondered if she should at least correct his choice of words but just hugged him. It was nice having someone on her side, even if she was missing the café, and her best friend!

It took three days before Laura came round, in the evening, holding a huge bunch of flowers, and an *iTunes* card for Josh. 'Can I come in?' she said, looking very uncomfortable. Tilly was secretly pleased but kept her face impassive as she moved aside.

'Like a drink?' she asked.

'Pink?' said Laura.

Tilly opened, then poured two glasses of Zinfandel and handed one to Laura.

'Look,' said Laura, 'I might as well get this over…here…' she said handing her an envelope. 'Five hundred and forty pounds. I calculated everything you had written in the book. To be honest, I don't know how you did it all - I have only been on my own for three days and I am completely worn out. Please come back - I had a terrible time.'

Once she had drank a glass of wine Laura was on a roll, Tilly didn't need to speak. 'Not only could I not get the order for the baker right, I burned two lots of tea cakes before realising the toaster was on the wrong setting. Both times it set the fire alarm off with a café full of customers.' Without taking breath she continued. 'Then, on the night you left, the washing machine started to make clunking sounds so I had to turn it off and get an electrician in. There was nothing wrong with the machine; he just found some pebbles someone must have left on the table. 'She took a sip of wine and continued, 'Then, the dishwasher started to froth everywhere and I couldn't leave till eight o' clock. I am completely worn out. Tilly, please, please come back, I promise I will never be like I was.'

'But why were you like that? It won't work if we can't talk to each other.' said Tilly.

Laura's shoulders slumped as she said, 'I know. I was horrible, I really am sorry. I think I was so frightened we wouldn't survive if I paid us more, so half the time I haven't been paying me at all. I think I was afraid we would fail.'

'And will we? said Laura. 'Seriously, that's terrible.'

'That's the funny thing,' said Laura 'I was so focussed on keeping all the details but I avoided accepting the idea we might be making a profit. Then, if I found any, I just convinced myself we needed it for something. But now, after you shaking me up, I have been to see an accountant and he has said we can afford to both be paid and have a small raise. And, as well as that, we can pay someone to come in for a few hours three times a week so you can have more time with Josh…and I will cover more…please, please come back Tilly.'

Tilly just laughed and offered her friend another glass of wine.

It wasn't till later that Tilly said thoughtfully to Josh, 'Wasn't it odd that the toaster was set wrong and the washing machine and the dishwasher all went wrong on the same day? Almost like divine intervention, maybe?'

'I don't think so,' said Josh, as he got up to go to bed, 'I call it PAYBACK.' As he left to go upstairs he popped his head round the door and said with his eyes twinkling, 'Oh Mum, if you see those pebbles anywhere in the café or the kitchen can you get them for me? I keep them for good luck!'

Annette Hayes

Strawberry Tarts

'Oh, Anne and I have been going for so long it has almost become a ritual,' sighed Joan to her granddaughter.

Sophie had called in after school for a cup of tea. Joan had been telling her that she and Anne had been shopping to have a look around, then gone to the café for a cup of tea and a scone, as usual.

'That's a funny word to use isn't it, Gran?' she said looking for the biscuit tin. 'Ritual makes it sound like something witches do, something a bit unpleasant'.

'Oh no,' said Joan. 'Not unpleasant, it's nice,' she added, then hesitated.

'But?' said Sophie laughing. 'Come on Gran, dish the dirt!'

'What a horrible expression,' said Joan. But she was smiling. She liked talking to Sophie. At sixteen she was one of the few members of the family who didn't either think she was going senile because she forgot the odd word, or checked that she was wrapping herself up warm. Surely at seventy-six she could be credited with remembering her own scarf, she thought. She looked at Sophie, who was still waiting.

'Come on Gran, what's the ritual?'

'Oh well it's nothing really,' she said. She didn't want to be disloyal. Not only that, Joan knew that Ellie - Sophie's friend, was also Anne's granddaughter and would be calling in on Anne now. Both girls called on their grandmothers every Tuesday evening before going off to the gym together. But she also knew that Sophie wouldn't let it go.

'Well you know Anne always picks me up in her car and we go out every Tuesday and we really get on, and I really appreciate it, especially as I can't get out a lot these days.'

'And?' said Sophie?

'I...I just wish sometimes we could do something else, maybe go to the garden centre. Or even have strawberry tarts instead of a scone; it's just always the same. It's not too much to have a strawberry tart now is it?'

Sophie laughed and said, 'Oh Gran, you are funny, why haven't you told her you'd like to do that?'

'Oh, I couldn't, she might be offended,' Joan said. 'She just drives there, then we go to the café and then she orders scones!'

Sophie, thinking, finished her third chocolate chip biscuit then said, 'You know Gran we had psychology today, and the tutor told us that if you keep doing the same thing then you keep on getting the same outcome.'

'Well, there you go then,' said Joan, 'we keep going to the same place and I keep getting a scone.' They both laughed.

'No Gran I didn't mean that. If I've got it right, it meant that if we keep doing or saying, or not saying like we always do, then we keep everything just the same and nothing changes.'

'Maybe you're right,' she said thoughtfully and started to clear away the tea things.

A little while later Sophie got ready to leave.

'Are you meeting Ellie?' said Joan.

'We'll meet at the gym,' said Ellie, 'She was late leaving because she is in a different group for psychology to me.'

'Oh well give her my love,' said Joan and closed the door.

꙳

Joan settled down to watch *Come Dine with Me* on the television. 'It's enough to put you off entertaining forever,' she thought, 'the nasty things that people say about each other.'

Then she started to think about what Sophie had said. Maybe I should suggest that we go the garden centre next week, she thought. Or at least say I want a strawberry tart.

Later, before she went to bed, she thought about Arthur. When he had been alive he was so helpful, took care of so much. A little voice in her head was also saying 'and maybe a bit bossy,' but she didn't want to listen to that.

Just before she fell asleep she decided she was definitely going to have a strawberry tart on Tuesday. It didn't happen like that though.

ò

The next Tuesday was fine and Anne arrived at exactly five to ten as always. They talked about their week as they went towards the roundabout.

Then Anne suddenly said, 'I was wondering Joan, perhaps you might like to go somewhere else this week?'

Joan was just about to say, 'Oh no, that's fine,' when Sophie's face, laughing, came into her head. 'What a lovely idea,' she said quickly, 'how about the garden centre for a change?' So that's what they did.

Then in the queue for lunch Joan positioned herself in front of Anne and said, 'I think I will have the macaroni cheese, how about you?'

It was while they were having coffee, not tea, due to Joan suggesting cappuccinos after lunch that they started to talk about their granddaughters.

Joan waited, hoping she wasn't in trouble but Anne just said, 'You know those girls learn so much don't they? Ellie was telling me that she had a lesson last week in psychology all about how some people try to control their world by controlling others. Can you imagine that?'

'Well I never,' said Joan, 'how interesting.' They were both silent for a moment, thinking and sipping their coffees companionably. Then Joan said, 'You know if we go to our usual place next week, I think I shall have a strawberry tart!'

Mike Freeman

If Music be the Food of Love

I am the first to admit I'm not clever. Don't get me wrong, I'm not a fool and I went to a good school though I was foolish to waste my time there. Since I left I've worked on building sites. Thing is, I'm not your usual brickie. I don't smoke, I don't bet and I don't drink. I've nothing against drinking but I don't like pubs. I don't like the noise and the ragging and the jokes. I've heard all before. I get a good rate of pay and I don't spend much on myself. I've got a nice house and I'd like a nice car, something like an MG Maestro, but you can't take a nice car to a building site so I make do with my old Ford.

I'm a good brickie and I like plastering, too. Not as easy as it looks, plastering. You've got to get the movement right; get the right rhythm. It's like music; and that's what I do like. I sang in the church choir as a kid and I loved it. I sing now in the 'senior' choir at the church. The tenor line; not a high tenor but folk say I've a good voice and I can carry a tune. I'm not all that good at reading music but sing me the tune and the words, even in Latin, and I can remember them. I'm on the note, on the tempo, steady and true, that's me. And, like I'm telling you, I love it.

Thing is, as a bloke gets a bit older, he starts to think about a missus. I'm not that good with girls. The bright ones take the Mick and the thick ones are, well, thick. I'm not bad looking. A bit stocky, I suppose, but it's all muscle. I used to play rugby - a good prop forward I was, but I got bored with the club bar side of things, same old stories, same old jokes.

I'd like to have a missus but before that I'd like to be clever. Not quick-clever or college clever; more understanding-clever. There's more to life than laying bricks or plastering walls. I read a lot, mainly books from the library. I listen to talks on the radio and I watch *'Horizon'* on TV but I still don't know. I wish I'd listened more at school. I just want somebody clever to talk to; someone with patience to answer my questions. I listen to the vicar's sermons but they just seem to say the same thing in different ways. I asked the choirmaster but he said he's too old to understand this world and he doesn't know what it's coming to, either. I suppose, if I'm honest, I'm a bit lonely.

Like I say, I'd like to have a missus but the women in the choir are all old and scrawny spinsters, even the married ones. Well, that was the case up to a month back. Then Debbie arrived. She's got a lovely contralto voice; and the rest of her is pretty good, too. Slim and a bit stately, I suppose. She's got this lovely hair - the colour of deep red bricks like Barton Brindles. I stand just behind her in the choir and I can look at it. I have to be careful; it makes me forget the music. New teacher at the High School, she is, English; comes from Cheltenham, degree from Oxford. By heck Bill, I said to myself. She's out of my league, I'm thinking.

Well, I had this solo bit in the anthem last Sunday and after the service Debbie turned round and told me how much she liked it and how she looked forward to singing each Sunday with me close behind her. And, we chatted as we walked out to the car park together and I felt she liked me. Well, I thought, bugger Cheltenham, I'll ask her for a date. Not just like that, I'm telling you. I thought she won't want a cinema or a pub. I put my best voice on and said would she like to have dinner with me one evening. Just like that, I did. And she said, yes, she would like and Tuesday would be nice. I was real taken aback. She told me where her flat was and I nipped back in to the choirmaster. I didn't think a pub or even a *McDonalds* would be her scene. I didn't tell him it was Debbie though I think he knew. He told me about this place in the next town, 'The Cock Door', and he fished out the telephone number from his diary. I'd heard of trap doors and fire doors but a cock door was a new one on me.

On the Monday morning, I rang up and booked a table for two like the choirmaster said and spent the next two days worrying. But she was ready when I picked her up. When we got there the place looked expensive but I'm not short of cash. It wasn't a cock door. It said *'Le Coq d'Or'* over the front.

Before I thought, I said, 'What's that mean, Debbie?'

'The Golden Cock,' she said. I looked at her sideways, I can tell you, but she didn't seem to be bothered. I thought, well, it's not a rude joke, then, but you can never really tell with the French.

Two, not one, two waiters took us to our table. It were a nice one by the window looking at a courtyard with plants in pots and things. They pulled out the chairs for us and pushed them in again as we sat down. They flapped open these big napkins and spread them across our knees.

'An aperitif, Madam?' or something like that, one of them said to Debbie. She asked for a dry white wine and I had my usual tonic water. Then the menus arrived! By heck, it were all in French! But Debbie wasn't a bit put out. I hit on a simple plan; I had what she had.

She talked about teaching; I talked about the choir mainly. It turns out this is her second job - she's Head of English - and at my old school! By heck, I thought, she's even further out of my league.

We had 'consommé' soup to begin with. I didn't expect it to be cold but Debbie didn't seem to be bothered. The main course seemed to be all vegetables. They were piled up in a big heap but arranged in a sort of pattern on the plate. The meat, a nice and tender bit of beef, was underneath it all. As we finished, one of the waiters sidled up and asked me how I found my beef. I told him, it weren't easy because it was hidden under the spuds and that there weren't that much of it when I got there. I looked across at Debbie for support but she had her face buried in her napkin. It was very tender, I told him, because he did look a bit shaken.

We had fruit salads for sweet because that's what we both like; and coffee afterwards. That was 'in the lounge' with little bits of chocolate. It seemed to go well, particularly for a first date and, back outside her flat, she leaned across and kissed me!

'Bill,' she said, 'You're priceless,' but I drove home a bit worried whether she was taking the Mick.

☙

I didn't say much to her at choir practice on the Thursday. We have four old biddies in the front line of the sopranos. 'The Trout Quartet', the choirmaster calls them; behind their backs. They come together in an old Ford Anglia one of them has. In the car park afterwards they were all twittering like sparrows. The 'church car park' doesn't really belong to the church and folk going to the pub across the road fill it up while we're in practice. Well, two cars had boxed it in, hadn't they? They couldn't open either of the doors. So I got behind it and put my hands each side of the boot and pushed. It was not easy but no worse than bump-starting a dumper truck. And they were mighty relieved. They all gathered round me after it and queued up for a hug and a kiss. You should get the handbrake checked, I told them. I looked round for Debbie. She saw me but she was talking with the choirmaster so I just went home. I'll see her on Sunday, I thought, don't rush things.

～

Well, at service this morning, I had her hair in front of me again, didn't I? So, in the last hymn, I floated the tenor line of '*Abide with Me*' just like silk and just past her right ear. She turned her head round after and grinned at me. It made my heart beat faster, I can tell you but there was more to come. In the car park she told me she's taken out a subscription to the Philharmonic and wants me to go with her to a concert this coming Friday. She wants to go with me!

I'm wondering if I can get my MG Maestro by then, anything better than my old Ford. I'm wondering whether I can talk to her about my questions. She's clever. She's been to Oxford University! I'm wondering what she sees in me. But she knows I'm only a brickie. It's all a bit worrying, really.

～

Well, all that was twenty-five years ago. Debbie and I celebrate our silver wedding next year.

But it turned out Debbie couldn't answer my questions either. 'Oh, Bill' she would say, 'that's Philosophy.' So I've read a bit of philosophy over the years. Let me tell you, some of those philosophers are stark bonkers - even when you can work out what they are on about. So I suppose I've stopped asking those questions.

I still sing in the church choir and I've still got Debbie's hair just in front of me. There's some grey in it now but I'll never get tired of it. I'm glad I wrote down the beginning of it all at the time. In fact, the only questions I have now are: What made Debbie come to this town and how come she just had to appear in front of me in the choir?

But again, I'm not really looking for answers. I'm just very, very thankful.

Mike Freeman

The Restaurant

Charlie felt intimidated. A *McDonalds* or even a *Little Chef* was his usual style and this place was not. It looked a different world but there seemed to be nowhere else. The commissionaire was large and uniformed. He had military medals on his chest and a waxed moustache on his upper lip. The entrance hall was also large with large mirrors and large dark wood furniture with large vases and large flower arrangements. There were even large chandeliers hanging from the high ceiling. The whole place was 'large'!

Charlie looked it over letting his eyes come to rest on the commissionaire.

'Smart little café, you've got here,' he remarked in a condescending tone. The large man was momentarily discomforted but regained his aloof composure.

'The Crystal Café is through the second glass doorway,' he intoned and added, after the slightest of pauses, 'Sir.'

'Excellent,' said Charlie, 'but where's the bog?'

The commissionaire inclined his head. 'Sir?'

'The Men's, the Loo, the Little Boy's Room, the Lav-a-tory,' Charlie spelled out.

The large man's moustache quivered. That the newly rich were often lower class, he knew but he also knew the establishment here could not afford to upset them.

'Through the third glass doorway,' he said and again added, 'Sir,' but after a longer pause.

'Right you are,' responded Charlie and strode down the hallway with as much swagger as his five foot six could muster.

The Commissionaire watched him, thoughtfully.

The third glass doorway revealed to Charlie a lavatory of cathedral dimensions done out in dark marble and gleaming brass. If he had not urgently needed a toilet already he would have done so at the sight of it all, the folded pile of hand towels, the larger pile of larger towels, the arrays of bottles and soaps beside the commodious basins - all of which he took in as he flung himself into the nearest cubicle.

His somewhat noisy defecation was followed by the usual feeling of exquisite relief but then anxiety returned to Charlie. How, he wondered, was he going to get out of this place? A small window beneath the overhead cistern made him consider an unorthodox exit. Alternatively he could wait until the commissionaire went off duty but Mary was waiting to continue their journey, waiting in the car outside - a Ford Fiesta he had parked at the side, out of sight of the main entrance.

He stood on the seat and looked out. By the greatest luck it was just outside. The trouble was that the toilet downpipe ran right in front of the little window and constricted the escape path. There was no alternative – he must run the gauntlet of the moustache and the medals. After all, there was not a lot the large man could do.

Charlie made full use of the basins, their accoutrements and towels while trying to revive his courage. He also offered up a silent prayer that the commissionaire be absent or otherwise engaged. Emerging, he found his prayer unanswered, the man was at his station. Charlie walked towards the entrance finding it difficult to avoid the eye of the large man who moved just an inch towards his path.

'Sir?' he said in that questioning way that is also threatening.

'Wrong address,' said Charlie, shaking his head woefully. The commissionaire looked unimpressed but held open the large door. As Charlie moved through it the large man let it go. It caught Charlie's backside and propelled him ignominiously onto the pavement.

As he picked himself up, Charlie thought that a little pain externally was but a small price to pay for his new-found comfort, internally.

Mike Freeman

The Volunteer

The rain drilled into the ground as the team sweated and heaved the heavy rails onto the sleepers they had laid the day before. As wet inside as they were outside they muttered and cursed in turn, conscious of increasing danger as the light faded from the hillside. Dislocated limbs were the least of personal tragedies on this line. The whole quarrying complex it served had a graveyard for the workers. Of course it was located well away from the mansions of the owners.

Andrew sweated and cursed with the rest. He included himself in his invective. He should have known better than volunteer for this, yet his options had seemed so limited. The ganger shouted again and the six-man team heaved in concert then straightened up for a breather while he ran the gauge stick over it.

'Pin it,' he shouted at last and three of the gang held it while Andrew and two others hammered the clench nails into the sleepers. Surely that was it for today? 'One more rail,' sang out the implacable ganger and the curses redoubled. The thought that he was wet through anyway did little to improve his mood or lift his weariness. At least he would be a 'holder' for this rail. Some of the gang could hammer with either hand but Andrew's right was aching from wrist to shoulder.

A flash of lightning with a Wagnerian thunder roll made him want to laugh. He stood to hold the rail expecting trolls and elves to appear from behind the trees. The assortment of attire sported by his co-workers would frighten them as much as them surprising us, he thought.

A slap on the back from the satisfied ganger brought him back to reality and the mood lifted as they all trudged back down the line to their cabin.

At least he had dry clothes there before his two-hour drive back to Birmingham and another boring week as a legal executive. Would he feel better if he had played rugby this weekend? No, he decided. Fifty yards of well-laid track extension for a heritage railway felt rather better than the chance of a cup in the cabinet at the clubhouse.

In any case, the rugby team option was a bit of non-starter now his girlfriend had left him to shack-up with the scrum half.

Mike Freeman

Mind Me

On the outside of me there is a world, a universe, deep space.
It is alien to me, my self, my inner self
where the words come and go, the ideas form and reform.
I am comfortable in myself.

I see you there, not here, but there on the outside;
on the outside of my world, my self where I'm so comfortable.
Will you disturb my comfort? Will you destroy my dreams?
And I dismantle yours?

You want to have and hold me, to love and scold me.
And in return for me to hold and mould you,
your inner world, your dreams, your comfort.
Will they will be mine to disturb and destroy?

What will happen when we lie together, when we lie to each other?
How can I tell you of the world inside me; the dreams I seek?
If you listen when I try, will you hear those words that come and go
or will you only hear the words I speak?

Can we learn to hear each other's silence?
Tread softly throughout each day and in the night?
The risk is great, the danger clear - and yet
hold me, dearest, hold me - but not too tight.

Mike Freeman

The Village Bonfire – A Writer's Elegy

Bright the light the flames provide with nothing more to aid one's eyes
to see the others standing there, their faces turned towards the glare
with dark all round they have no form, no solid shape to hold the frown
or laughter that each face portrays like masks upon the drama stage.

Thus is concealed the inner fears we have for those of tender years
whose moving sparklers fool the eyes to see bright circles in the dark
from whirling hands thought safe in gloves and happy smiles
of those well loved, not yet bedazzled by the lights of restless city.

They still can find on earth a paradise enabled by the light
from spark and flame to eye and eye and into minds
which, till they die like embers in that ash tomorrow, will hold the image
of one night, one brightened night, through all their sorrow in this life.

For each one has a brief of time in substance like the dancing fire
that burns for us to give the view that we believe or not believe
there is some meaning in the light to calm and save us
from the terror of the night that waits behind us, watching without pity.

Yet in this here and by this now we make our choice and with our voice we
mask our fear and speak to each and join the laughter of this feast and
stand our ground with those around who stand beside the fire, the love of
light and fear of void reflected in their eyes.

We all so think that in this glow before we go our words
will also stand and dance and sparkle in the memory and so
we write about the things we see within the light of brightened night
and thus upthrow, from this our life, a leaping height to immortality.

Helen Barratt
Julia

February 21st. Her birthday. Every year on this day he would go upstairs to the attic to spend time with her. He would go to the furthest corner of the dusty room and, because it was always dark in there, he would light a candle and place it in the special candlestick.

Was that her voice? 'All the better to see you with, my dear!' Whenever they had lit candles, mainly at their intimate suppers, she had said those words, and laughed teasingly.

Now in the gloom of the attic, he followed his imposed rules, as he did every year on this date. His little ritual, his homage to his darling Julia. He shivered. The attic was icy cold, but the flickering, true light of the candle gave him some comfort, if not warmth. He noticed that the skylight window, which let in only a little light at the best of times, was framed by an inch or two of fresh snow. Through the little window he could just make out the dark fingers of the old oak against the steely sky.

He crossed to the trunk in the corner and opened its heavy lid. There, her picture! He gasped at the sight of her. It happened every year, her beauty would take his breath away.

'Julia. My love, my own darling,' he whispered.

He sat in the old rocking chair, just gazing at her picture in the candlelight. The portrait was of a woman in her thirties, leaning against a tree - the old oak in their garden. She was wearing the lilac dress, his favourite, and holding her straw hat. Her hair was moving with the breeze and gave the picture the appearance of Julia being carefree and happy. She was happy then and he knew she was a woman in love. In love with him.

He held the candle nearer to the picture so that he could study the detail of her auburn curls and teasing smile. But, as always, it was her eyes that held him. Velvet brown eyes, laughing back at him.

He stopped rocking. 'My God Julia, you can still do it. You still possess me...you always, will – won't you my darling?'

After a time he stood up and placed the portrait on a little table nearby. He went back to the trunk and took out a silk shawl, the ivory shawl Julia wore in the portrait. He rippled the fine material through his hands and fingered the beading and intricate embroidery. Exquisite. He remembered the first time Julia had modelled the long shawl, just for him. She had draped it about her naked body and only let him open his eyes when she was in the right position.

'Do I please you, sir?' She had laughed provocatively, she could torment him with a glance. She had seemed like an angel to him then, with its folded wings. Yet an angel who had the devil in her – who could entice any man she wanted with those eyes, that smile.

He pulled the shawl over his head, like an enveloping shroud. Ah, yes, he could just still detect the faint trace of her perfume. He closed his eyes and sat back on the chair, rocking to and fro, to and fro.

.....He hummed softly to himself. Julia's song. He could not remember the words now but this was the tune that Julia sang whilst busying herself about their home. So many years ago now. It seemed like a dream sometimes, and Julia like a ghost.

❧

He awoke, still in the chair, some time later. Startled, he pulled the shawl from his head and stood up. Was that the sound of a bell he could hear, or was he dreaming?

The attic was now almost completely dark apart from the light from the candle, which threw dark shadows about the walls. He shivered. Through the skylight, he could just make out large snowflakes falling silently.

So it was over for another year, his birthday visit to Julia. Carefully, he folded the shawl and put it back into the trunk. Picking up the portrait, he kisssed Julia and held her to his breast. Then he placed that, too, back where it belonged.

'Happy Birthday, darling Julia.' he whispered. 'You will never have to grow old like me, will you my dear?' He put away the candlestick into the trunk and closed the heavy lid. As he moved wearily towards the stairs, led by the light of the candle, he could hear the bell again.

He sighed. Esme would be wanting her evening meal. If she did not get her food at the time specified on her chart, she was inclined to panic.

He went downstairs, took a deep breath, and although nobody could see him, he smiled patiently. He blew out the candle's flame.

'Just coming, my dear, just coming.'

Helen Barratt

Up, Up and Away

'Tea, coffee or hot snack, Madam? Anything from the trolley?' The stewardess smiled at Mary.

'No, thank you...I'm fine. Nothing for me.'

Mary sat back in her seat and closed her eyes. She wasn't used to flying on her own. She noticed her hands were shaking a little. Nerves, or excitement?

Usually, by now she and Roger would have had the conversation about how wonderful it was to be flying off somewhere, after all the planning and the preparation. Then there would have been the next part, where Roger would recount - loudly and at length - the history of the particular aircraft in which they were travelling and also a detailed specification of its engines. Mary would sit there, exclaiming in all the right places, whilst mentally searching for something intelligent to ask as a question. Most of the time she failed miserably and would just nod in all the right places.

That would normally go on until the refreshments were served, or until Roger fell asleep. Mary knew better than to interrupt him whilst he was in 'full flow'. Roger was a knowledgeable man, he could discuss most things and took pleasure in doing so, and often.

Thinking back on trips they had shared made Mary realise that they were not really holidays. They were more like...expeditions. Roger was an expert on Ancient Scriptures and lectured at the University. Professor Roger Radcliffe, such a grand title.

They had visited Jordan, Syria, Israel and many other places in the Middle East and beyond. Once at their destination they would travel out daily to obscure places which had meaning for Roger, but not his wife. They would travel for hours across desert locations, sometimes without seeing another human being all day. All they needed, Roger insisted, was their hired jeep, food supplies, lots of water, a good map and intrepid spirit. Who needed other people, he would say. They had each other and his work. But sometimes the Professor did not remember to speak to his wife all day.

Oh, how she had longed to just sit by the hotel pool and lose herself in a book. Now and again, she would feign illness - a sick headache, a touch of food poisoning, perhaps and reluctantly Roger would allow her to stay back for a day. Those blissful days, just pleasing herself and chatting now and again to other guests. Perhaps even flirting a little with the waiters.

Mary would have liked to have visited popular holiday places such as Spain, Italy or Greece. To have a holiday with no agenda, no plans. She would have liked to have tried paragliding, have a go on a pedalo or just have fun. But she knew Roger would not have liked that.

The other volunteers in the charity shop where she helped out, thought she was crazy going to locations which they could not even pronounce, let alone want to visit. Mary liked the charity shop well enough, but she was only there two afternoons a week. She often imagined what it must be like to work in an office, have a career and hold down a responsible position.

Roger had not wanted her to work outside the home when they married and at the time, she felt that he was being protective of her. He had told her he wanted to take care of his new wife, it was a man's responsibility.

Mary thought back now on the years wasted on keeping the house pristine, just as Roger wanted, not a cushion out of place, everything perfect for when he came home from the University. She remembered how he used to look around the living room and she would wait for him to nod his approval. If there was something he did not like, he would not speak to her for the rest of the evening. Silence, save the ticking of the clock for company.

Sometimes he would write a note for her and place it by her pillow for her to read the next morning. But not a love note. It would be a list of tasks he wanted Mary to do again, to meet his approval and to be ready for his return that night.

Her parents had been somewhat alarmed that Mary's education, whilst not a University one like Roger's had nevertheless been solid.

They had made sacrifices for their only child, and now it would be put to little use. However, they felt that perhaps Mary would pass on her skills and knowledge to their future grandchildren.

Ah, Mary thought. The next generation. Well, that was never going to happen now, was it? She was fifty-four and she and Roger had no children. Roger had never really shown any interest in having any, he said that his students at University were enough for him. They had never discussed it further.

Sitting there with her eyes closed, two tears ran down Mary's cheeks. One for each of her unborn babies, she thought. Babies which would only ever live in her heart. Anyway, Roger hardly touched her any more. After the first few happy years of their marriage, he only seemed to become excited about the latest historical finds. He often hinted that he thought intimacy was for those of lesser intelligence and why would they need that?

She wiped away the tears. Who am I, she thought. I am not a sister, nor a daughter any more - I am just Roger's wife. That is all. She turned the wedding ring on her finger. I am just Roger's wife. A nobody.

But not anymore! This is my time, she thought. All those years, sitting alone at home whilst Roger was at the University, she had planned for this day. Her escape. She had taken in translating jobs and had taught children privately. She had good skills with languages, especially Spanish. She had come top of the whole year in the exams at school and her tutor had said it had been a pleasure to teach her.

So week by week, month by month, she had squirreled away money she had earned and topped it up with a little from the housekeeping that Roger gave her. She banked online and this saved any statements coming to the house. Slowly, the amount had built up until she knew it was time.

Carefully, she had hidden a few clothes away. Not new clothes of course. Roger thought that fashion was frivolous. So she bought a few of the better offerings which came into the charity shop. After some attention, they could pass for new. She had stored them in her mother's old trunk in the loft. Roger had no interest in the trunk and had been disparaging about Mary's 'little treasures' as he called them. He thought the only contents of the trunk were her childhood mementos, her old school books and diaries.

So, leaving him a note when she left the house this morning was completely appropriate, she thought, just like Roger always did.

'Roger, by the time you read this, I will be far away. I do not love you - and probably have not for a long time now. Oh, you may love me, in your own strange way. But how would I know, you never show me. Anyway, it does not matter any more. Do not try to find me, concentrate on your ancient manuscripts. I want my life back...Goodbye.'

Mary smiled as she remembered placing the note on his pillow this morning. She looked at her watch. They would shortly be arriving at Palma.

Leaving her seat, she went down the aisle to the toilet and went inside. Without another thought, she took off her wedding ring, threw it down the pan and laughed as it flushed noisily away.

Chris Stork
The Mad Queen of the Pier

On the last day of Nora's holiday, the house was unusually quiet. Herbert sat cross-legged on the wooden floor in a sea of crumpled up notepaper, glaring at the brooding, abandoned grand piano. It was as if it was calling to him, pleading in its gruff piano voice - *'Come on, play me…play me…'* or more likely it was taunting him - *'Call yourself a musician, Herbert!'* He chewed on his knuckles and pulled on his earlobes, cursing his lack of inspiration. The deadline for the completion of his commissioned soundtrack for the upcoming television documentary, *'Coastal Curiousities of Ceredigion'*, was looming fast. Herbert decided he was rapidly descending into madness.

Nora looked up from her book and glanced at the clock. The time, as time does, was slipping away, never to return. Her uncle was still wearing his crumpled pyjamas. He looked like a wild beast, pale, tormented and unshaven. She was restless, though not bored. She could never be bored here because she loved to spend her days exploring the shadowy spaces of Herbert's old house. In the hallway, there lurked a snarling, stuffed pole cat, ready to pounce. Carved, wooden tigers prowled on the mantelpiece, paintings of white horses galloping through clouds and gloomy portraits of people from long ago, hung on the walls. There were drawers, full of things that rattled and musty cupboards containing fossilised trilobites, precious stones from South America, and purple genie bottles from Egypt. In the attic, she had found fearsome Indian masks that made her shiver and leering Toby Jugs lurked on window sills. Her favourite discovery was the winking ventriloquist's dummy who lived in a red, velvet box in the cupboard beneath the stairs. She had named him Boris, and liked to tell him all her secrets. She whispered about the bullies at school, and showed him her drawings of monsters and her collections of driftwood and sea glass. Sometimes, she sang him a little song or read him a silly story she had written. Whatever she said or did seemed to make him grin rather vacantly and roll his eyes.

Nora looked out of the window and sighed. It was a grey, silent kind of day. The wind was too cool to go into the garden and up into the tree house. Inside, there was a glimpse of the distant bay and she could sit for hours watching the changing light dancing on the sea. She tapped a rhythm on the table top and began to drum with her fingers.

'Nora, please don't do that.' snapped Herbert.

'Sorry.' She tried to concentrate on her book. It was a good story - about a girl who ran away with a unicorn, but Nora's restlessness was growing.

'Uncle Herbert...'

'Hmmm?'

'Please could we go for a walk on the pier?' Herbert's frustration hung like black curtains around the room. 'I have to go home tomorrow and school starts next week.'

Herbert stared at his little niece, thin as a stick insect with her freckled face and inquisitive brown eyes that hid behind pink glasses. He shook his head in disbelief. She looked so forlorn.

'Tomorrow?' He sighed. 'I'm so sorry, Nora - I haven't been much fun this week, have I?' He glanced at the piano. *'Play me...play me'*...it commanded. His heart sank. He looked back at Nora's face. 'You're right, we should go out.' He stood reluctantly and stretched. 'I'll get dressed.'

Nora was thrilled. A walk on the pier with Herbert was a special treat and each year it was great fun.

'Come along now, young Sticklet,' her uncle would say. 'I'm going to fatten you up,' and, pulling a monster face, he would raise his arms, turn his hands into twisted claws and growl, 'and get some meat on you before I eat you alive!' And she would scream and run ahead to escape through the raised archway at the entrance of the pier with Herbert lumbering close behind her.

She loved the small fairground with its bobbing, carousel horses. Better still were all the delicious smells that came drifting to tempt her. Herbert would buy her a candyfloss or a donut or sometimes an ice cream with a chocolate flake. At the *Hook a Duck* stall, he would applaud with passion if she could catch one of the yellow, swirling ducks to win a giant, furry monkey which always lost an eye by the end of the day. Serenaded by rock and roll music, they'd take a ride on the dodgem cars and Herbert would put one arm protectively around her shoulder and steer with the other. And sometimes she was allowed to take the wheel and inevitably they would smash into another car.

'Did you know, Sticklet, that you are probably going to be the world's worst driver - ever,' he would tease, before ushering her into the *Hall of Mirrors*. There she would look on with wonder at her amazing, zigzag legs and bulbous arms and Herbert's face would grow as large as a football, his untamed, red hair a long triangular flame growing out of his head.

※

But this day on the pier was rather different. They walked the in silence, past the fairground, past the shuffling crowds in their plastic macs and the pensive crab-fishers and the rows of empty deck chairs. This time they didn't pause to watch the outrageous antics of Punch and Judy. Instead, Herbert took Nora's hand and they ambled on till the distant, shrill cries of the puppets and the voices of the shrieking children carried like a dream on the wind.

They had never ventured this far. They came to the seasick-orange Sunset Pavilion and peeped inside to see a beaming man in a dazzling suit pumping out a tune on his Wurlitzer. He began to sing, '*When marimba rhythms start to play, dance with me, make me sway, like a lazy ocean hugs the shore, hold me close, sway me...*' His voice echoed around the vast, empty ballroom and Nora tapped her feet, strangely thrilled as she studied the sequinned couples who mamboed and twirled across the lonely dance floor.

※

They walked on and on, pausing for a while to to watch the lazy sea slap against the barnacle-ridden, wooden piles, then on past a couple of lovers whispering and kissing to the sad strains of an accordion, played by an old man in a black coat and bowler hat.

'We should watch for dolphins,' said Herbert and from his worn jacket pocket he pulled out a pair of binoculars. Nora screwed up her eyes but all she could see was a fishing boat and far in the distance, a large ship anchored in the bay. She looked at Herbert, standing there, tall and pale in his horn-rimmed glasses.

'Uncle Herbert,' she said, tugging on the sleeve of his jacket. 'What can you see?'

'Well - not a lot actually, Nora. These binoculars are broken.' He looked down at her with a very serious expression. 'But watch out...' He pointed to the ship. 'I think that be a pirate boat out there. And, it be heading this way!' And half-heartedly, he added, 'Shiver me timbers - arrr!'

'Don't be silly!' she giggled, delighted that Herbert was attempting to make her laugh. She'd heard people in her family, talking in low voices. 'Our Herbert's a bit mad, you know...' Nora didn't care what they said. Didn't they know that Herbert was the funniest man in the world? Anyway, at school, the bullies whispered things about her, too. They said that she was weird and they pushed her over and tripped her up. She tried not to care. She knew she was different to them, but she wasn't really sure why. Even so, the thought of returning to school filled her with gloom.

☙

At the very end of the pier, they paused to look back at the little seaside town. It seemed so far away, like another world in another time. Here, the structure felt forlorn, detached and deserted. Herbert seemed to sink into deep thought, standing for a long time, staring out to sea as if Nora wasn't there. The greyness of the day hung like a veil across the bay and the cloud seemed to be growing thicker and darker.

Nora suddenly became aware of a strange, metallic sound and turned to see some crumbling stone steps. She made her way down to another level of the pier where there was a rusty, green shack with faded letters that read, 'The Olde Aqareum'. Hanging from the building, creaking as it swung to and fro in the breeze was a badly painted sign of a laughing, pink octopus. The place looked lonely and unloved and Nora would have retraced her steps, but Herbert had appeared behind her. He frowned, intrigued, and gestured that they should take a look.

Inside, the darkness was pierced only by a miserable light bulb and the eerie, green glow of a large tank in the centre of the room. Nora held her nose to keep out the stench of rotting fish and worried that the sinister bubbling sound might be coming from a vat of horrible remains.

'That'll be two and six,' demanded the old woman who stepped from the shadows. She turned to leer at Nora though the gloom and her breath smelled of dead things.

'The kid can go free.' With rising terror Nora tugged at Herbert's arm.

'Uncle Herbert...let's go.' But he reached into his pocket and pressed the half crown into the woman's greasy hand.

'We'll just have a look at the sea creatures, Nora,' he said, with an air of defiance and they stepped warily into the shadows to peer into the murky waters of the slimy tanks.

'There's nothing there,' she said. 'Let's go.' But there was a sudden movement and a small crab shot into view before disappearing into the mud. And that was it. The empty tanks bubbled and yellowing neon lights flickered on and off.

'Excuse me,' called Herbert. 'These tanks are empty. Could we have a refund please.'

The old woman was indignant. 'Empty? Well, take a look at that!' She pointed to a solitary fish swimming in the tank in the centre of the room. 'His name is Winston.' She grimaced in a spine-chilling way. 'I call him King Cod.' The enormous fish swam round and round, eyeing them with disdain.

'That is indeed a fine specimen of a cod...' said Herbert. The woman slid up close to the tank and Nora saw her face, green and distorted, peering through Winston's watery domain.

'When I sell this place, he's going to the Sea Breeze.'

'Ah, excellent - so he'll be housed in another aquarium?' asked Herbert, raising an eyebrow.

The woman snorted. 'That ain't no aquarium - that's my brother's chippy!' She tapped her dirty fingernails on the side of the tank. 'He never uses that frozen muck.'

Herbert stiffened. 'Come along Nora,' he ordered.

'Wait, wait - there's another room yet...' The old woman stepped forward and gripped his hand. 'It's in the back.' She ushered them forward and lifted a curtain of sticky, plastic seashells.

As the light clicked on, Herbert and Nora stared with disbelief at the sign above the small, spotlit stage.

'The Incredible, Dancing Crab Quartet ,' he announced slowly.

'Two o' clock dayly,' read Nora, straining to see the sign which had been scrawled in pencil on a piece of cardboard. She looked at her watch and shrugged. 'We're just in time.'

'Ah, yes, sorry about that,' said the woman. She threw the cardboard sign to the floor, unwrapped a toffee and put it into her mouth. She spoke with difficulty as she chewed. 'It's Friday. Their day off today.'

'Day off,' said Herbert, nodding his head. 'I see.'

'Ah, but wait till you see *'The Mermaid Show'*.' She rubbed her hands together and promptly disappeared behind a grubby sheet which doubled as a curtain. There was a peculiar, metallic scraping as a heavy object was dragged slowly across the floor.

'Ouch,' they heard the woman groan in pain. 'Damn this sciatica,' she cursed. Within seconds Herbert and Nora heard the crackling of a scratched, gramophone record. The tiny, damp room was filled with the sounds of a storm with lashing seas and a booming, distant fog horn. Suddenly the curtain was pulled back to reveal a rusty, tin bath, over the end of which hung a large, rubber fish tail. They stared in shock at the old woman, dressed in a long, blond wig, covered in strands of seaweed and draped in a fishing net. As she began to wail like a banshee, Herbert grabbed Nora firmly by the arm and pulled her swiftly out. They stood blinking and gulping in the cool sea air.

'Diabolical,' said Herbert, his face flushed with anger. He glared at Nora. 'Just...diabolical!' Nora looked as if she had just seen a ghost. And then Herbert began to laugh. It was a deep, infectious laugh that grew into a roar that seemed to ring out across the waters of the bay. Soon, Nora was laughing with him, giggling so hard that big tears fell down her cheeks.

'Dear me, dear me. That was just unbelievable!' gasped Herbert, leaning against the railings, pulling a handkerchief out of his pocket to wipe his eyes. He struggled to stand up straight, and Nora rubbed her aching sides and coughed.

'Come along, Sticklet,' said Herbert, glancing at the dark sky. 'We should be getting back.' He reached out and ruffled her hair. 'We could have chips for dinner - but I don't think I fancy a fish.'

'Definitely not fish,' she agreed. 'Ever again.'

As they walked slowly back along the pier, Herbert would occasionally shake his head with disbelief and snort with laughter and Nora too would burst into giggles. Glancing back at that strange, green shack she imagined a proper seaside aquarium filled with interesting things. Then, she had a very big idea.

'Uncle Herbert, when I'm grown up, we could turn your house into a museum of the seaside.' Herbert stopped and turned to face her.

'A most excellent idea, Sticklet!' he said. He took her hand and shook it hard. 'Congratulations!'

'We could call it, *'The Old Museum of the Sea.'*

'Yes, yes, I love that! But what might we put into it?'

Nora had dozens of suggestions and began to count them out on her fingers.

'Proper fishes in proper tanks...sharks' teeth...tins of crab eye jelly...bottles of sea mist...an old sea captain with a big, grey beard...a treasure map...a jar of shipping forecast...a dancing jellyfish...some of my drawings of sea monsters, and of course - a pirate's plank...' She smiled at Herbert. 'And, you could dress up as a pirate with a wooden leg and play sea music on the piano and I could sing whale songs and tell people stories about storms. Oh, and I'd look after your parrot and teach it to say poems about shipwrecks.

Herbert, who had been listening intently, put his hands on her shoulders and stared down at her. 'Do you know what, Nora?'

'What?' she asked shyly. 'Do you think I'm mad?'

'Exactly that!' he said, with great tenderness. 'You're as mad as I am. You could possibly be *even* madder. Who cares?' Nora suddenly remembered what the bullies had said to her and a worried frown etched itself across her face.

'Sometimes, it's good to be mad,' Herbert assured her. 'Though we're not really *mad* - we're just *different* from everyone else, us mad people.' He drew a big circle with his arms. 'You see, Nora, we have big imaginations, and without us, the world would be a very boring place. We are here to open our minds and dream, discover our potential and create great sculptures and paintings, design wonderful buildings and bridges, write poetry and stories and amaze people with our songs and our plays and our dances...' He grimaced, 'And, ...create music that will live on and on.' Nora understood clearly and she nodded and her frown began to fade. 'In fact,' said Herbert, 'we are very special.' He stroked her hair. She liked the idea of being special. Suddenly the bullies didn't matter any more and she looked at Herbert with eyes that shone with enthusiasm. As if by magic, the beginnings of a melody flashed into his mind.

'Nora, you have brightened up the day,' he said and he scooped her up and placed her on his shoulders. Riding piggyback, from up on high, Nora looked out to sea with a deep sense of happiness. I am the Mad Queen of the Pier, she decided, and she gave a regal wave to people passing by.

And the gulls seemed to scream their approval, and the dolphins leapt out of the bay and even the sun came storming out of the clouds, wrapping Herbert and Nora in an ethereal light that stayed with them till they reached the end of the pier.

Out in the bay, the setting sun was resting on the horizon and the old house seemed to glow in an amber light. Herbert sat at the piano and Nora sat by his side, thrilled to see his fingers dance, once again, over the keys. The simple melody he'd been humming all the way home had now been embellished and embroidered and had grown into an extraordinary piece of music, curling round the room, evoking images and sounds of westerly shores, ebbing tides and a lonely sky. Nora closed her eyes and dreamed of floating away.

As the final note faded into the dying light and the piano seemed to sigh with contentment, Herbert sat quietly for a moment. Then he turned to her.

'I hope you liked that. I'm calling it, 'For Nora.'

'Thank you,' she whispered.' It was beautiful.'

He smiled, took the child's small hand and kissed it gently. 'No - thank *you*,' he said.' 'Thank you, Nora.'

And for a long time they sat together, holding hands in the darkness, two silent shadows looking out at the restless moon. Only mad people can do this, thought Nora.

Brian D. Roberts

Garrulous Hoardes

Forming and reforming to the rhythmic sweep of
nature's baton, a million chattering starlings
jostle and jockey against the evening glow.

Garrulous hordes, mantled in shot silk and
sprinkled with pearls, swirl in night black
tumultuous clouds against a setting sun:

slowly melting into the swaying reeds and the
fretful silence of the marsh.

Contributors

Sandra Johnson lives in a jungle on the edge of a forest with four ducks and a husband. Her latest novel, 'Angel Orange,' is an e-book available from Amazon and is a magical story suitable for children age eight to ten.

Trevor Bell is a consulting psychologist who likes to write horror and ghost stories in his spare time. He lives in Cheshire with his wife, has two married children and is a grandfather.

Anne Abbinnett is a retired primary school teacher, who, when she isn't walking her dog or having long conversations with her cat, can be found on hands and knees weeding her flower beds.

Doug Barratt is living in Cyprus but continues to be 'involved' in the group from a distance. His interests include genealogy, air transport, West Ham United FC, 60's music and the recent history of Cyprus.

Lynne Stokoe's beloved family and many friends are uppermost in her life. She likes music, theatre, festivals, the sea, happy endings (of which there are too few in real life), but most of all to be useful.

Peter Scarisbrick formerly worked in the chemical industry and since retiring has been able to indulge in the pleasure of writing fiction. He is fascinated by the magic of where stories come from and the characters who populate them.

Christine Milliken grew up in Buckinghamshire and trained as a teacher in Cheltenham. She enjoys reading sci-fi and fantasy books. She loves life but doesn't take it too seriously and believes this is reflected in her writing.

John Edwards draws comfort from what those he has known have given him, and what he has given them. He is afraid and lost in the world of technology and cyber space. His spiritual food is a warm word, a caring look and a loving hug. His warmest memories all involve the people he has known and still knows.

Annette Hayes lives in Chester with her husband Ian and her little dog Maisie. As a psychotherapist for over twenty years, when she writes she likes to focus on her characters and their relationships.

Mike Freeman has studied physics and philosophy, religion and commerce. He maintains that love and laughter outplays them all.

Helen Barratt lives in Cyprus with her husband. They have two grown-up children. Retired from teaching adults and management, her interests include singing, art, crafts, reading (mainly fiction) and writing. 'Live, laugh, love. Then write about it!'

Chris Stork has a background in community arts and theatre in education. She feels privileged to have worked in a variety of settings with groups and individuals of all ages and abilities. She loves walking the dog, wild places, film, theatre and the absurdities of life.

Brian D. Roberts One of the group's founder members, Brian passed away in 2011 and is sadly missed. He is remembered as a big man with a big heart and a great sense of humour.

Lightning Source UK Ltd.
Milton Keynes UK
UKOW04f1917151214

243194UK00005B/511/P